APR 2 1 2017

computational
Fairy Tales

computational
Fairy Tales

Jeremy Kubica

Cover design and art by Meagan O'Brien
Interior design by Marjorie Carlson
Set in Bell MT, Gill Sans,
WWDesigns, LogoStile, and ChopinScript

Dedication

To my family

Contents

A Note to Readers

THIS BOOK FOCUSES ON computational thinking. The stories are written to introduce and illustrate computational concepts. As such, they focus on high-level concepts, the motivation behind them, and their application in a non-computer domain. These stories are not meant as a substitute for a solid technical description of computer science. Instead, these stories are meant to be used like illustrations, supplementing the full concept.

The book covers a range of material, from introductory programming through more advanced algorithmic concepts. The stories are organized into sections by concept. Each section covers progressively more advanced concepts.

Finally, each story is meant to (approximately) stand alone. While most of the stories follow Ann's quest to save the kingdom, there are multiple side stories that are disjoint from the main thread. All of these stories take place in the same kingdom.

Major Characters

Ann is the teenage daughter of King Fredrick and heir to the throne. She has been tasked by the prophets with rescuing the kingdom from the coming darkness. Unfortunately, the prophecy was very vague about the specific threat facing the kingdom.

King Fredrick is the king and Ann's father. He is a wise, fair, and occasionally lazy ruler.

Marcus is a powerful wizard and staunch friend of the king's. He is a firm believer in the importance of the practical aspects of magic, such as testing and commenting.

Clare O'Connell is the kingdom's brightest computational theorist. She spends her days working at the Bureau of Farm Animal Accounting: Large Mammal Division, where she has assembled a talented team of theorists.

Peter is an apprentice at the Library of Alexandria and an eager, though occasionally arrogant, student of computational ideas.

Sir Galwin is the king's trusted head knight. He has years of experience with difficult quests.

The Start of a Quest

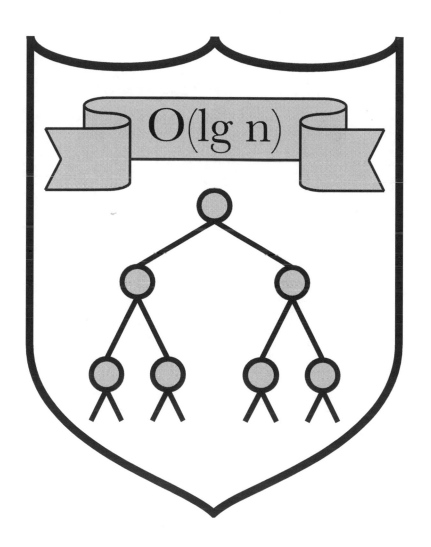

The Darkness is Coming

"**T**HE DARKNESS IS COMING," stated the seer.

He was the fifteenth seer to stand in front of King Fredrick this week. Fifteen seers—all with the same prophecy. Darkness. Chaos. Doom.

Granted, each seer brought his or her own twist to the prophecy. One spoke of "ill winds" and added a small shiver for effect. Another shouted loudly about the "end of times" until he was forcibly removed from the room. A third gave the prophecy as a malformed limerick, causing everyone in the room to wince at each attempted rhyme.

In contrast, this seer was much less dramatic; he was calm and to the point. Princess Ann liked that. She had never been a fan of unnecessary theatrics, especially in prophecies.

Of course, Ann didn't care for the message itself. Why did the kingdom have to be doomed? Things were going really well for her. Now some horrid "darkness" was going to consume the lands.

As her father began to cross-examine the seer, Ann idly wondered how many seers were left today. She tired of the constant proclamations of doom. Why not intersperse a minstrel or two? Anything to lighten the mood would be welcome.

"Ann?" asked King Fredrick in a loud voice. He stared at her. Ann realized that he was waiting for an answer, but she had no idea what the question had been. She had stopped paying attention after the initial prophecy.

"I'm sorry. What was the question?" she asked.

Ann heard a few surprised gasps from the back of the room. Her father sighed and looked at her crossly.

"Will you take on this quest? Will you go forth and save the kingdom?" he asked.

Ann froze. What quest? Why her? And why was Sir Galwin, the land's most famous knight, glaring at her? He should be beaming at the mere mention of a quest. He loved quests.

"What quest?" Ann asked.

"To travel forth and find a way to stop the darkness," responded her father. He spoke slowly, as though to ensure Ann was paying attention. It reminded Ann of how he ordered his breakfast in the morning—her father left no room for misunderstanding in some aspects of life.

Ann rather liked the suggestion of a quest. She longed to travel the kingdom, but had never been allowed. With the summer holidays starting next week, this quest sounded like a wonderful opportunity. She might get to see the famed upside-down pyramids of South Patagonia or the great Library of Alexandria. Her father even supported it.

"Sure. I can do that," she answered quickly.

"It will be a long, lonely, and dangerous journey," her father added. "But you must find a way to save the kingdom and hold back the darkness. The prophecies have said you must travel forth alone to find the answer."

"Wait, what? Alone?" sputtered Ann. They never assigned solitary quests to teenagers. Usually a first quest involved a whole platoon of veteran knights. She didn't know the first thing about questing.

Her father sighed again. "Did you listen to any of the prophecy at all?"

"No," Ann admitted. "I stopped listening when he reached the you-are-all-doomed part. I've heard that a hundred times already. It gets boring."

Everyone in the room stared incredulously at her. She started to feel uncomfortable. She briefly wondered if she could somehow escape.

"I see," her father began. "In short, the seer said that you can save the lands. You need to go find a way to stop the darkness, or we are all doomed. Then he said something about Fortran being the one true language. Honestly, from that point on it was incoherent."

"But... alone?" asked Ann.

Her father gave her a serious look. "Alone."

Ann nodded numbly, and again wished that she could run out of the room.

After that, there might have been more said. There might have been cheers or mumbled messages of luck. Her father might have given words of encouragement. The seer might have provided more information. However, Ann didn't hear anything else. The entire room faded from her mind as her new responsibility dawned on her.

❧

Computer science is inherently a way of thinking about problems. How can you route pieces of information across a distributed network that spans the globe? How can you render pictures that look more realistic? How can I get this stupid program to stop crashing?

The answers to these questions build on a set of core concepts—approaches to solving fundamental problems in computer science. This book focuses on these core concepts, the problems they address, and how the concepts can be combined to solve even larger and more complex problems.

An Algorithm for Quests

An algorithm is a set of specific steps or instructions for solving a problem. For example, there are algorithms to sort numbers, compute mathematical results, and render images.

❧

A NN STARTED TO PANIC as she packed for her quest. How was she going to find the answer and save the kingdom? She rarely traveled out of the capital city, and even then she had never gone beyond Millington. Now she had to search all the known lands for a way to save the kingdom. It quickly dawned on her that she had no idea what she was doing.

Her thoughts were interrupted by a sharp knock on the door. Sir Galwin stood rigidly at the entryway, looking mildly uncomfortable.

"Sir Galwin," Ann greeted him cautiously. He had been sulking since Ann had received her quest, and she was afraid of setting him off again.

"I came to wish you luck," Sir Galwin offered. "I'm sure you'll be successful in your quest."

"Thank you," replied Ann.

The knight nodded a stiff acknowledgement and turned to leave.

"Sir Galwin, do you have any advice for me?" asked Ann before he could go.

The knight turned back toward Ann. From the wide smile on

his face, Ann knew that she had asked the right question. Sir Galwin loved to share his stories about quests almost as much as he loved questing itself.

"Follow the established algorithm for quests, and you'll be fine," Sir Galwin assured her.

"An algorithm?" asked Ann. She had never heard of an algorithm for quests. Hope flowed through her. She could handle algorithms.

"It's simple," started Sir Galwin. "If you have one or more leads, you follow the best one. Otherwise, if you don't have any leads, you travel to where you can find more information. Break any ties by flipping a coin."

This advice surprised Ann. She didn't know what she had been expecting, but this certainly wasn't it. It took her a few moments to figure out how to voice her confusions.

"This approach seems to involve a lot of guessing," ventured Ann.

"I prefer to think of it as a heuristic," said Sir Galwin.

"A heuristic is basically an educated guess—a rule of thumb, if you prefer," said Ann. "Is there anything more exact? Something without any guessing, perhaps? Something that guarantees that I find a solution quickly?"

Sir Galwin let out a deep throaty laugh. "I said the same thing when my mentor described this approach to me. I resolved to develop a better algorithm for solving all quests."

Ann waited for him to continue, but Sir Galwin appeared to be watching a pigeon outside her window. As far as Ann could tell, the pigeon was not doing anything particularly interesting. It paced along the window ledge, bobbing its head.

"Did you?" she finally asked.

"What? Oh. The algorithm. No. I never invented anything better. I eventually realized that the established algorithm was pretty good. It turns out that quests always involve some guessing."

"So my entire plan is to keep following the best lead and collecting new information?" Ann confirmed.

"Yes. I call it the Information Maximization for Issue Resolution algorithm," said the knight. "I think it sounds much better than what my mentor used to say. He would call it 'figuring stuff out.'

"Think of it as a search for an answer. At each step you try to either move closer to the answer or learn more about the problem itself. Hopefully, learning about the problem will help you find an answer."

"How do I figure out the best lead? How do I figure out where to get more information?" asked Ann.

"You have to find a strategy that works for you," said Sir Galwin. "I rank things according to a gut feeling. I use 0 to indicate 'feels utterly normal' and 10 to indicate 'feels wrong.' For me, a 10 feels similar to eating three pounds of refried beans. I also use a special data structure to track everything. That system saved my life hundreds of times. One time, I was hunting a particularly nasty bog dragon through some marshlands—"

"Is there anything else I should know?" interrupted Ann. She was desperate for any more information.

Sir Galwin thought for a moment. Finally, he said, "Avoid chasing bog dragons through marshlands."

For the twentieth time this hour, Ann wondered what she had gotten herself into.

Variables and Magic Gifts

A variable is a place in memory where you can store a single piece of data. Each variable is associated with a name. Programmers can reference, modify, or set the value of a variable using its name. Variables can also have associated types, such as integer, Boolean, or float. These types indicate what kind of information can be stored in the corresponding variable.

❧

A NN MADE IT LESS than two miles from the castle before the crushing weight of her task once again descended on her. The fate of the kingdom depended on her finding a way to stop the darkness, yet she didn't know what it was or even how to find out. She felt utterly alone.

Ahead of her, Ann saw a man walking up the road wearing a bright blue wizard's cloak with silver threading. She instantly recognized Marcus; no other wizard dressed so fashionably. He was also one of the kingdom's most powerful wizards and a staunch friend of her father's. If anyone could help her in the quest, he could.

"Sir Wizard!" she called out to him, embarrassed that she had never learned the proper etiquette for addressing a wizard.

Marcus looked up with a smile. "Princess Ann. How are you this lovely morning? Out for a ride, I see."

"Unfortunately, I'm not," responded Ann. "I'm embarking on an important quest. The seers have predicted a coming darkness, and I must stop it."

"Alone?" asked Marcus. His smile vanished.

"Yes. The prophecy said that I 'must journey forth alone to stop the coming darkness.' But … perhaps you could still join me. Technically, we met after I had already journeyed forth alone. In fact, I've been journeying alone for about two miles. And, I could really use your help," Ann pleaded.

Marcus shook his head. "That wouldn't be a good idea. Prophecies are fiddly things, and they don't like it when you try to find technicalities. One time I thought I found a loophole in a prophecy; as a result, it rained Haborian Slugs for three days. It was terribly messy. You must go alone."

Ann's heart sank. Tears started to well up in the corners of her eyes, but she fought them back and nodded bravely to Marcus. She knew he was right.

"Maybe I can still help you, though," continued Marcus. "Let me see what I have with me." As he spoke he rummaged through a small pack. After a moment, he extracted a couple of curious looking objects.

"I have with me some of my latest magical works," he explained. "They're based on variable magic."

"Variable magic?" asked Ann. "What's that? And what happened to your other work?"

"I'm taking a break from all plant-related magic for a while. A terrible accident with roses," Marcus said without further explanation. He trailed off, and Ann thought she detected a hint of anger in his expression.

He shook his head as though clearing a horrible image. Then he continued, "Variable magic is a useful, but often overlooked, form of magic. It's based on the simple idea of storing values. Take this rock for instance. It uses what's known as a 'location' variable."

"What does it do?" asked Ann, her eyes wide with interest. After algorithmic design, magic was her second favorite conversation topic.

"Stores a value, of course," answered Marcus. "Weren't you listening? It stores a location."

"So, you could use it to ..." Ann paused as she thought. She couldn't think of a single use case.

"You can use it to find your way back to a given place," Marcus finished. "For example, you could hide treasure and use the rock to store its secret location. Or you could store your current location before heading into a dangerous bog, so you can find your way out. Or you could use it to find your horse in a particularly large parking lot. It has many practical, everyday uses."

"I see," acknowledged Ann. She silently wondered what Marcus's "everyday" life must be like.

"You simply tap the rock with your index finger five times," explained Marcus. "Then the rock will store your current location in a magic variable. No matter where you are, the rock will continue to point toward the saved location until you set a new one."

"Like a compass?" asked Ann.

"Exactly!" exclaimed Marcus. "Except you set the location instead of it always pointing north."

"It can only store a single location?" asked Ann.

"That's how a variable works; it only stores one piece of information," answered Marcus. "Think about a small pocket—you can fit one thing in it. You can change what you have in it, but you can never have two things in it at the same time."

"I guess it would depend on the size of the pocket," commented Ann.

"Tiny, tiny, tiny," responded Marcus. "A tiny pocket that can only fit one thing."

"Oh. Well, thank you." said Ann. She was still uncertain about the actual usefulness of a compass rock.

"I also have this for you," said Marcus, handing her a small coin purse with a counter on the front.

"A purse?" asked Ann.

"A *magic* purse," corrected Marcus. "It works like a calculator. It uses a variable called 'value' to track how much money the purse contains. This purse displays that amount on the front.

"When you put a coin in, that amount is added to the 'value' variable, and when you take a coin out, the appropriate amount is subtracted from 'value.' It always tells you how much money you have in the purse."

Marcus demonstrated the concept by inserting a nickel into the purse. The counter on the front increased by five cents. Ann imagined a magical variable within the purse changing as the result of the addition.

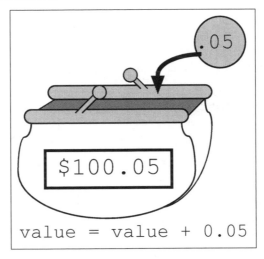

"Why would I need that?" asked Ann. "I can always count the money."

"Ah," said Marcus with a smile. "Counting takes time. What if you're in a hurry?"

"I see. Thank you again for these wonderful gifts," Ann responded with false enthusiasm. She already knew that the gifts wouldn't help her.

"I hope they help you on your quest," replied Marcus. Then he quietly added, "If I had known you were departing on a quest, I would have brought better magical items for you."

He shrugged, closed up his pack, and prepared to leave.

"Sir?" ventured Ann. "May I ask you for one more favor? Do

you have any advice to give me on my quest? Any helpful pointers on where to start?"

Marcus paused for a long moment and looked off into the distance. "I don't know what the darkness is, or where you should go. I'm sorry. Instead, I'll leave you with the following advice: don't get eaten by a dragon. I hear it's terribly unpleasant."

With those words, Marcus continued his journey toward the castle. He hummed to himself as he went.

Once again, Ann felt a pit of despair in her stomach.

The IF-ELSE Life of the King's Turtle

IF-ELSE statements allow programs to branch off and execute one of two different blocks of code. The **IF** statement starts by evaluating a Boolean (true/false) clause. If this clause evaluates to true, then the block of code conditioned on the **IF** statement is executed. Otherwise, it is skipped. An ELSE clause can be included to provide an alternate block of code in the cases where the original Boolean clause evaluates to false.

F IDO, KING FREDRICK'S PRIZED pet turtle, lived a charmed life. He spent his days in the garden fountain, swimming and sleeping. He didn't have any magic powers, aside from the ability to amuse himself for an hour by staring at a pebble, but King Fredrick was quite fond of him. Due to his quiet nature and lack of razor-sharp teeth, Fido had always been Ann's favorite pet as well. The castle's servants took good care of him. They made sure that his fountain was always mostly clean—Fido did enjoy the occasional patch of slime.

Fido lived by a series of simple rules. In fact, since his brain was roughly the size of a pebble, they were incredibly simple IF-ELSE–style rules. These rules made up Fido's entire daily routine. For example, he had simple logic to determine when he ate:

```
IF he was hungry then he ate
```

This logic worked well for Fido, because he ate when he was

hungry. And, as a natural consequence, he didn't eat when he wasn't hungry. It was quite a good system.

For some aspects of life, the If statement could have two different actions depending on the condition. For example, when he was swimming:

```
IF the fountain is on then play in the fountain
ELSE swim around the large rock
```

Obviously, Fido enjoyed the fountain more than the rock.

Sometimes the decisions would be complex enough to require a series of chained IF-ELSE statements:

```
IF it is sunny then sit in the grass
ELSE IF it is warm then go swimming
ELSE sleep
```

On sunny days, Fido would happily sit in the grass. When it was warm but not sunny, Fido would swim in the fountain. And on those rare days when it was neither warm nor sunny, Fido would sleep. He hated those days.

The gardener responsible for taking care of Fido often joked that "All that turtle does is eat, sleep, and swim," which wasn't far from the truth. The logic that ruled Fido's life consisted of about fifty different actions contained within chained and nested IF-ELSE statements.

When Ann was a child, a visiting scholar had once spent a week studying Fido. With Ann's eager assistance, he recorded the entire logic for Fido's routine on a single scroll of parchment. If Fido had been intelligent enough to understand what that meant, he might have been offended. Instead, he sat in the grass—it was sunny.

Then, five days after the start of Ann's quest, the unthinkable happened. The gardener, worried that Fido would be bored without Ann's visits, added a second large rock to the garden. This addition threw off Fido's IF-ELSE–based routine completely. It took almost a full week for Fido to determine a new routine. In the end, he added another IF-ELSE:

```
IF he is closer to the right rock then swim around the
right rock
ELSE swim around the left rock
```

Thus order was restored to his life.

Loops and Making Horseshoes

Loops, such as the FOR loop or WHILE loop, are programming constructs for repeating a set of instructions until some termination criterion is met. Two primary things define a loop: 1) What you do inside the loop, and 2) the conditions to stop looping.

H UNDREDS OF MILES NORTH of the capital, in the small outpost of Garroow, the blacksmith Drex was losing his patience. His new apprentice, Simon, wasn't working out. In fact, Drex had never had a worse apprentice in his thirty-five years as Garroow's master blacksmith. Simon could barely lift the hammer, let alone swing it with sufficient force to shape metal. However, worse than that, Simon also lacked the necessary intelligence to carry out even simple tasks. Had it not been for his diminutive size, Drex might have thought that Simon was actually an ogre.

Drex found himself constantly repeating instructions:

"Now, hit the metal again."

"And again."

"And again...."

Drex's patience was wearing thin. He hated repeating himself.

Finally, Drex decided to try an experiment. "Simon, hit the metal twice," he commanded.

Clank. Clank. Simon complied.

"Now, turn it over and flatten it," Drex commanded.

Simon flipped the deformed-looking horseshoe and hit it once. Then he paused and looked back at Drex, confused.

Drex sighed loudly. Was that really too much for Simon to handle? The boy was hopeless.

"It's a loop!" shouted Drex. He knew that Simon wouldn't understand, but at least shouting made Drex feel better. "A simple, simple loop."

"A loop?" asked Simon.

"Haven't you ever heard of a loop?"

Simon shook his head sadly.

Drex realized that they had hit the core of the problem. How could Simon function as a reasonable blacksmith without understanding how loops worked? Then again, Drex had no idea how Simon could function as a *human* without understanding loops.

"A loop is defined by two things: something to do and a way to know when to stop doing it. You keep doing that one thing over and over until you stop," Drex explained calmly, reciting the favorite description by Garroow's famous scholar Dr. Whileton. Of course, Dr. Whileton tended to repeat himself, so he would have explained it at least a few times.

Simon stared back blankly.

"Think about a one-mile race," Drex suggested. "You run around the track until you have gone a mile. That's four laps, right? So, running is the thing you do and having run a full mile is how you know when to stop. The track even looks like a loop."

"I run until someone tells me to stop," said Simon.

"Of course you do," muttered Drex.

"In this case," continued Drex, "I want you to keep hammering that horseshoe until it's flat. As soon as it's flat, you can stop. WHILE the horseshoe is not flat, hit it with the hammer."

"Okay," agreed Simon happily. He promptly set about hitting the horseshoe over and over again. By the end, Simon breathed heavily from the effort, but he had succeeded in flattening the horseshoe.

Drex was stunned. How had Simon understood that?

"Good. Now go get the coals hot," Drex commanded.

Simon looked confused again.

Drex sighed. "It's another loop. Pump the bellows 10 times. FOR each number that you count from 1 to 10, give the bellows a pump."

"Okay." Simon again got to work, pumping the bellows exactly ten times. He counted loudly each time:

"One ... two ... three ... four ... five ... six ... seven ... eight ... nine ... ten."

Over the course of a week, Drex determined that Simon would repeat tasks if they were well specified in a loop. Drex would tell Simon exactly what task to repeat and exactly how long to repeat it. Sometimes he told Simon to count up to a certain number. Other times he phrased the command like a WHILE loop, telling Simon to continue doing something until he had met a goal.

Simon responded well to these structured commands. The blacksmith's shop was filled with the noise of Simon cheerfully counting and hammering. "One ... *bang* ... two ... *bang* ..."

Eventually, Drex introduced nested loops, issuing instructions such as "WHILE the sword is not thin enough, turn it over and FOR each number from 1 to 5, hit it with the hammer." Simon would happily go about banging the sword into shape while turning it over after every five hits.

Unfortunately, this formalized approach only worked to a point. Disaster finally struck when Drex tried to teach Simon more complicated computational concepts. As Drex and Simon stood outside the burning blacksmith's shop, Drex admitted defeat. Before leaving town for an open blacksmith's position in New Athens, he found Simon a better job—counting laps for runners on the local track team.

The Town of Bool

Boolean logic is based on two values: TRUE and FALSE (or alternatively ON and OFF for physical transistors). Complex logical expressions can be formed by using a few simple operations, such as AND, OR, and NOT. These expressions allow computers to perform logic such as adding binary digits, determining whether an IF statement executes, or controlling when a loop terminates.

❦

T HE TOWN OF BOOL was home to one of the kingdom's most respected logicians, Ellis Conjunctione. Ann had decided to visit the kingdom's scholars in the hope that they would provide insights into her quest. Unfortunately, upon arrival, Ann was informed that Dr. Conjunctione wouldn't be seeing anyone.

"I am sorry, but Dr. Conjunctione is busy at the current time," stated one of Dr. Conjunctione's graduate students. His voice projected a rare combination of formality and boredom. It reminded Ann of a over-practiced lecture, during which the teacher struggles to maintain his own interest in the material.

The graduate student stood in front of the university's doors, physically blocking Ann's path. He crossed his arms. Ann wondered if the student thought that pose would make him look menacing. In reality, he just looked uncomfortable.

"I'm on an important quest," insisted Ann.

The student appeared unswayed. "Dr. Conjunctione is already working on the single most important problem facing the kingdom: a logic problem called 3-SAT. Your quest will have to wait. He gave me explicit instructions not to be interrupted by anyone."

Despite arguing her case for two hours, Ann couldn't convince the student. He refused to compromise at all. Finally, she admitted defeat and resolved to move on to the next name on her list. She decided to stay the night in Bool before continuing.

Ann found her short stay in the town of Bool most annoying. She had always heard that the Booleans were strict believers in binary logic—everything was either true or false. She had naturally assumed that this simply meant that they were opinionated. For example, she wouldn't expect anyone in Bool to state "Jazz is *okay*." Opinions would be definite. However, she hadn't expected this philosophy to apply to absolutely every single aspect of life.

The first surprise came at a local restaurant.

"May I get more water, please?" Ann asked a waiter.

"No," he replied. "I only refill a glass if it is empty AND you're still eating."

"I *am* still eating," Ann assured him.

"But your glass is NOT empty," he responded as he moved off to the next table.

Ann looked down at her glass. It contained at most three drops of water. Ann sighed and finished those drops in preparation for the waiter's return. She decided that in this case she was going to embrace the Boolean philosophy and NOT give him a tip.

Luckily, Ann was well equipped for her stay. She had studied Boolean logic as an elective in kindergarten. It all came down to a few simple rules:

- There are only two options: TRUE and FALSE,
- A **AND** B evaluates to TRUE if and only if both A and B are TRUE,
- A **OR** B evaluates to TRUE if either A or B (or both) is TRUE,
- **NOT** A evaluates to TRUE if and only if A is FALSE.

The logic matched how people used the terms in everyday life. Unfortunately, though, the laws of Boolean logic weren't designed for living everyday life.

Over the course of her 16-hour stay, Ann continued to experience the frustration of dealing with the Booleans' world. She found that when the park "closed at sunset," the patrons would stay until the second the sun dropped below the horizon and then run out of the park. Similarly, getting directions turned out to be extremely aggravating.

"Is the hotel in that direction?" she asked, pointing approximately southeast.

"It is NOT in that direction," proclaimed a Boolean on the street. "It is in *that* direction." The Boolean pointed in almost, but not exactly, the same direction. Ann sighed and walked in approximately the correct direction.

"You are NOT going in the correct direction," the Boolean shouted after her. Ann ignored him.

She also resolved to program Marcus's compass to guide her back to the hotel. That way, if she went out, she could avoid having to ask for directions again.

Even the signage in Bool was overly logical. The crosswalk light actually said "Cross when the WALK light is on AND there are no cars speeding toward you." Did they really need to clarify that? Ann wondered what would happen if someone misprinted the sign to use an OR. Would it be chaos?

Ann only fully understood the Booleans' true adherence to this logical formulation when she reached the hotel. There, on the back of her hotel door, was a fire escape plan like you would find at any hotel—except, in this case, all of the conditions were specified as long Boolean logic statements. "Use the south stairs IF (they are NOT on fire AND the north stairs are on fire) OR (there is an obstruction in the hall toward the north stairs) OR ..."

After reading the sign four times, Ann decided that in the event of a fire she would be too confused to escape. She promptly resolved to leave Bool as soon as she could.

Unhappy Magic Flowers and Binary

Binary is a number system in which each digit can take one of only two values: 0 or 1. Binary allows the computer to encode information in a series of switches that are either on (1) or off (0).

Each binary digit represents a power of two. The first (right-most) digit represents the 1's place, the second digit represents the 2's place, the third represents the 4's place, and so forth. For example, the binary number $10110 = (1 \cdot 2^4) + (0 \cdot 2^3) + (1 \cdot 2^2) + (1 \cdot 2^1) + (0 \cdot 2^0) = 22$ in decimal.

<hr>

T HE DELIVERYMAN PAUSED OUTSIDE of the wizard Marcus's New Athens townhouse. Marcus smiled. He had recently returned from visiting King Fredrick in the capital, and he was waiting for the backlog of missed deliveries. There should be at least five important potion ingredients and a new hat arriving today.

Yet the deliveryman didn't continue toward the door. He stood transfixed, staring at the flowers. After two minutes, Marcus went outside to see if there was a problem.

"Your flowers have changed since yesterday," observed the deliveryman. "I'm sure the one on the right was red yesterday. Today it's blue."

"Those are the same flowers," responded Marcus. "Some of them are sulking today. Stupid flowers."

"Sulking? Do flowers sulk?" the deliveryman asked.

"Actually, it's more of a protest," clarified Marcus. "They are, of course, magic. They protest whenever it doesn't rain. It's quite aggravating, really. I water them every day, yet they still insist on sulking."

"Huh?" The deliveryman looked back and forth between Marcus and the flowers, trying to make sense of Marcus's statement.

"They protest by changing color to blue. Roses are supposed to be red. You have probably heard all of the poems to that effect, 'Roses are red' and such. But these roses insist on telling me how long they have had to 'suffer' without rain." Marcus gestured angrily at the roses as he spoke.

"They talk to you?" The deliveryman took a step away from Marcus.

"Of course not. They simply change color."

"What does color have to do with when it rained?"

"Well," started Marcus. "they used to all change color together after three days without rain—a sort of mass protest. Then they started to organize. They want to let me know exactly how unhappy they are. So now they count the days."

"Only two are blue," observed the deliveryman. "It hasn't rained all week."

"Nine days, to be exact," corrected Marcus after looking at the flowers. "They use binary."

"Huh?"

"Red flowers are zero and blue flowers are one," Marcus added.

That explanation did not help. In fact, it seemed to further confuse the deliveryman. However, on the positive side, he no longer looked as though he wanted to run away.

"Binary?" prompted Marcus. "Each flower represents a different digit, and thus a different power of two. The rightmost flower means one (2^0), the one next to it means two (2^1), the one next to that means four (2^2), and so forth. Add up the numbers represented by the blue flowers and you get the total number of days. Right now only the first ($2^0 = 1$) and fourth ($2^3 = 8$) flowers are blue, so it's been $2^0 + 2^3 = 1 + 8 = 9$ days."

The deliveryman looked. Sure enough, the five flowers across

Marcus's porch were: Red Blue Red Red Blue (or 01001).

"Why do they use binary?" asked the deliveryman.

"They tried to spell out the numbers on their petals, and they got too confused. So they had to settle for each flower being either all red or all blue. It turns out that flowers aren't that smart. Binary is a simple enough system for them. If they were smart enough for anything else, do you think they would be complaining to me about the rain? There's nothing I can do about it!" Marcus shouted the last part directly at the flowers.

"But how do they work together?" The more absurd the story got, the more interested the deliveryman became. He leaned in toward the flowers.

"It's really quite simple for them to count in binary," started Marcus. "When it rains, they're all happy and turn red. They effectively reset the counter to 00000. I like those days a lot.

"Then, each morning all of the flowers wake up and decide what color they'll be for the whole day. If it hasn't rained, they increase the count.

After 1 day: Red Red Red Red Blue (00001 = 1)

After 2 days: Red Red Red Blue Red (00010 = 2)

After 3 days: Red Red Red Blue Blue (00011 = 2 + 1 = 3)

After 4 days: Red Red Blue Red Red (00100 = 4)

After 5 days: Red Red Blue Red Blue (00101 = 4 + 1 = 5)

and so on.

"You see, each flower looks to its right in order to decide what to do. If its right-hand neighbor changes from blue to red (1 to 0), then the flower flips its own color. A blue flower changes to red, and a red flower changes to blue. This keeps happening until one of the flowers doesn't change from blue to red."

"What about the right-most flower?" asked the deliveryman. "How does it know what to do?"

"Ah. *That one is the instigator*! I'm sure he's the one that started it. Every morning there's no rain, he flips. He's the one that starts the process off. Red to blue to red to blue."

The deliveryman thought about it. "Why does a flower only change when its neighbor flips from blue to red?"

"Think about it the way that you would count with numbers 0-9. When you hit 9, you can't go any further with that digit. So you increase the next digit by one and roll the current digit back to 0. It's like going from 19 to 20 or from 29 to 30. Only here there are exactly two options for each digit, 0 and 1, so things roll over more frequently."

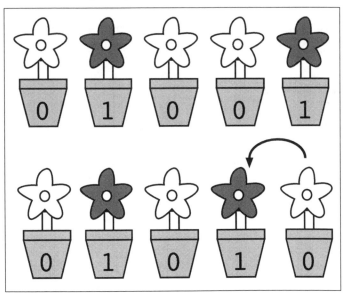

"That system always works?" interrupted the deliveryman.

Marcus tore his attention away from the right-most flower. He suddenly wondered how the discussion had gone from a rant about magic flowers to counting in binary. Did the deliveryman not have any other deliveries? For that matter, where was the delivery for Marcus?

"Yes. They've already counted out nine days, haven't they?" answered Marcus flippantly.

Then, seeing the look of interest on the deliveryman's face, Marcus returned to his teaching tone. "Consider what happens if doesn't rain tomorrow. The first flower will switch from blue to red, so the second flower will switch from red to blue. The count will go from $01001 = 9$ to $01010 = 10$."

The deliveryman looked impressed. Marcus couldn't understand why. The flowers were really annoying.

The Importance of (Variable) Names

Writing 'readable' code is vital to the long-term usability of the code. Code that is clearly written is easy to understand (both for the original programmer and for future users), easier to maintain, and easier to check for mistakes. One important aspect of readable code is the use of clear, meaningful variable names. Using meaningful variable names can greatly improve the understandability of code.

❦

B Y THE TIME PRINCESS Ann reached the northernmost outpost within the kingdom, she was losing hope. Her father, King Fredrick, had sent her on a quest to save the kingdom from impending darkness weeks ago. So far, Ann had found nothing.

The outpost of Garroow had been hit particularly hard by the chaos. The frequency of goblin attacks had increased in recent weeks. The commander, Sir Aat, had sent word to Ann's father that the outpost desperately needed reinforcements. At a loss for better stops on her quest, Princess Ann headed north to Garroow. While there she also hoped to consult with the world's second-most expert in loops, Dr. Whileton.

Ann found the situation in Garroow worse than she had expected. First off, Dr. Whileton had left for Guelph to start an "important collaboration" with another loop scholar. Nobody could provide details on the project or the timing of his return. Second, and perhaps more importantly, the outpost itself teetered on the verge of collapse.

During her first night at the outpost, a small goblin attack almost overwhelmed it. The fifty-person garrison barely held off three relatively tired goblins. She heard the captain shouting orders at his soldiers:

"Ut, guard the south wall. No, I meant Ot. Ut, stay where you are.

"Drex—no, I mean Dex—swap places with Plex. We need an archer on the wall, not a blacksmith.

"Et, secure that door."

Eventually, the soldiers repelled the attack and put out the fires. However, the lingering feeling of chaos and confusion continued to bother Ann. It worried her that the garrison's response had been so disorganized. It was like watching her father's turtle Fido try to chase its own tail. The problem wasn't the number of soldiers in Garroow, but rather how they were being commanded.

Ann resolved to fix the situation before leaving the garrison. She spent the entire night pondering the different algorithmic strategies, certain that one of them would help the garrison run more efficiently. As she had been taught from an early age, almost every problem has an algorithmic solution. Ultimately, the true problem dawned on her at 3 a.m., and she fell asleep confident that she knew how to fix the situation.

"Sir Aat," she addressed the commander at breakfast the next morning. "We need to discuss the attack last night."

"Yes," agreed the commander. "The goblin threat is real. Now you see why we need the reinforcements?"

"No," responded Ann.

The commander looked shocked. The rest of the dining hall fell silent. Everyone waited to see what Ann would say next.

"You need better names," Ann continued.

The commander laughed deeply. "You don't understand. We've already improved our names. When a soldier joins the outpost, I assign him a new name. Every name is short so that commanders can call out orders quickly in battle."

"No," disagreed Ann. "It's inefficient."

"No offense, Princess Ann, but what do you know about commanding in battle?" he asked.

"Only what I observed last night. But from that limited introduction, I can assure you that the names are hurting your efforts."

"I think you're mistaken," declared the commander. "They allow us to issue commands at incredible speeds."

"Yes, they do," agreed Ann. "But they're prone to mistakes. Last night, you corrected yourself 89 different times. The names are too similar and thus too easy to confuse. Plex and Dex. Ut, Ot, Et, and Aat. The short names don't help!"

"Ha! What would you suggest?" scoffed the commander.

"Use descriptive names. For example, Plex should be called 'South Tower Archer' or at least 'Archer Plex.' That more accurately reflects his role."

"That's crazy!" bellowed the commander as he slammed his mug of coffee on the table. His anger at being lectured overrode his manners toward the future ruler of the kingdom. "Do you know how long it takes to say 'South Tower Archer' in the heat of battle? We would waste valuable time."

"Do you know how long it takes to say 'Dex, swap places with Plex, we need an archer on the wall, not a blacksmith'? Any measure of efficiency needs to take into account the time spent on corrections," Ann countered.

"Well—you see—our old blacksmith Drex recently relocated, so—" started the commander.

"What about you?" Ann interrupted. "Why not have them call you 'Commander' or 'Captain'?"

"Our names already reflect rank," replied the commander. "The names proceed down the ranks in alphabetical order. It allows any soldier to instantly know who outranks them! It makes life simple!"

"No it doesn't. In order for the soldiers to refer to each other, they have to learn new, made-up names. Why not have them learn the ranks instead? Either way they have to learn something new. Only, in this case, the ranks mean something."

"We have a good system!" argued the commander.

Ann sighed. "It's like programming a complex algorithm," she explained. "Using short variable names can make it feel more efficient to program, because you can type out the code faster. But, in the long run, it can do more harm than good. It becomes easy to make mistakes and difficult to sort out what's happening. Oftentimes, slightly longer names can make a significant difference."

The commander opened his mouth to argue but couldn't think of a rebuttal. Instead, he sat at his table, mouth open, with a confused look on his face. After a while, he spoke.

"Princess Ann, I think you might have a point." Secretly, the commander also felt a small pang of relief. He had never been fond of his own assigned name. He often found himself daydreaming of his soldiers saluting and shouting "Yes, Commander!" in unison.

That afternoon, the commander changed every soldier's name to be longer but more meaningful. Over the next few days, the troops stumbled through drills, getting used to their longer names. But soon Ann began to see efficiency improve.

A week later, on Ann's final night in Garroow, goblins attacked again. This time the invading force consisted of ten highly trained goblin special-forces troops. The Garroow soldiers turned away the attack with ease.

As Ann left the garrison, she took a small bit of pride in the dramatic improvements in the forces there. After indulging in the brief moment of happiness, she turned her horse south and continued on her quest to save the kingdom.

Pseudocode for the Quest Algorithm

Pseudocode is an informal way of writing algorithms in order to make them easily understandable. While it represents actual computer code, it does not adhere to the syntax of any programming language. Instead, it is often written as a mixture of programming syntax and natural language.

A S SHE RODE, ANN pulled a small scrap of paper out of her bag:

```
WHILE I have NOT stopped darkness:
    best_lead = "Find new information"
    FOR each lead in my list of leads:
        IF lead is better than best_lead
            best_lead = lead
    Follow the best lead
    Check if I have stopped the darkness
```

She already knew it by heart. It contained the algorithm that Sir Galwin had taught her. Despite its simplicity, looking at the algorithm always gave her hope.

So, without any leads, Ann picked a new city in which to gather information. She would travel to Guelph and consult the foremost expert in loops, Dr. Iterator. With any luck, she would also find an opportunity to speak with Dr. Whileton.

She carefully folded the paper and returned it to her bag. At least she had a plan.

Data Structures

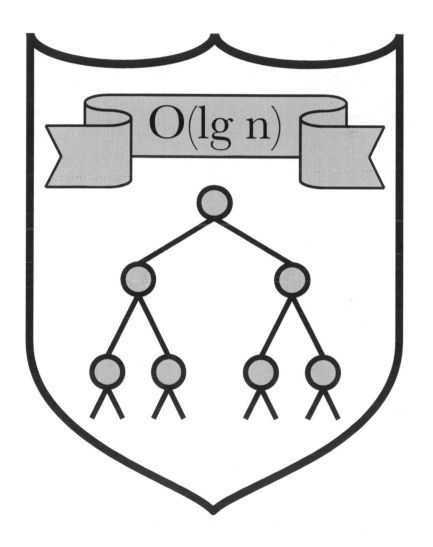

Arrays, Linked Lists, and Zed's Coffee

Arrays and linked lists are both simple data structures that store multiple values in memory. These data structures differ in how they store and allow access to the data.

Arrays are like a set of bins with a fixed number of slots. Their structure makes it easy to read from or write to an arbitrary element in the array.

In contrast, linked lists are easily expandable chains of data. However, you must scan to the correct location in the chain to read or modify a piece of data in that node.

⚜

O NE YEAR AFTER ZED opened his coffee shop in the capital, business was great. Zed had a devoted set of regulars who bought coffee every morning on their way to the castle. They were mostly bureaucrats, specializing in such jobs as counting the kingdom's cattle or copying maps. King Fredrick's steward had become a particularly devoted patron, drinking an alarming amount of coffee each day. Even Princess Ann used to frequent the shop before she departed on her quest.

Then, one day, a competitor opened shop across the street. Zed started losing business to MegaCup's low prices and flashy signs. Zed knew he had to expand.

Looking over the books, Zed noticed that he sold a lot of coffee in the morning but almost none at night. None of his customers wanted to be jittery as they headed home and went to sleep. Zed needed a new product—something he could sell at night.

His supplier told him about a new type of coffee coming from the southern region of the kingdom, "Low-Jitter Coffee." Immediately, Zed knew this coffee would solve his evening sales slump. He ordered eight cases.

Zed needed a way to market his new coffee. The sign outside his store read "Coffee" and didn't have room for anything else. After a week of intense thought, Zed ordered a new ArrayDesignBoard menu board for outside his shop. The board had four slots into which you could slide the menu items you wanted to display. He slid in "Coffee" and "Low-Jitter Coffee" tags.

The new coffee became a huge success. Zed's business doubled in a week. He added four baristas to the evening shift. He even attracted a few new morning customers, such as the king's tailor, who had long ago learned not to mix sewing and strong coffee.

However, Zed's competition soon caught on. A week later, Zed noticed a new shingle on MegaCup's sign: "Low-Jitter Coffee." The war was on.

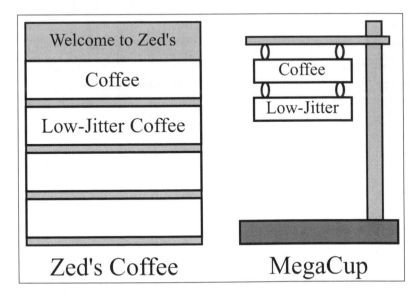

Then his supplier told him about another type of coffee. Called "Double-Bold Coffee," it was significantly stronger than the normal brew. A single cup could keep you awake all night. Zed ordered eight cases and a new menu tag for the ArrayDesign-Board menu.

Again, the new coffee became a rapid success. His morning crowd loved it. The steward alone ordered three extra-large cups each morning. Zed also started attracting new customers from the castle's night guards. They needed something strong to keep them awake during their watch.

Alas, MegaCup soon added a new shingle to the end of its sign.

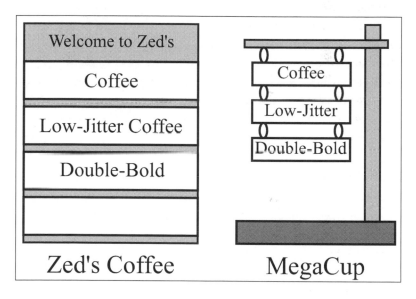

The next time his supplier visited, Zed grilled him on the other types of coffee available. After obsessing over the supply lists, Zed decided to try a novel approach. He ordered one case each of ten different flavors. He put these flavors into a rotation, constantly offering new variety.

This rotation approach worked particularly well with Zed's sign. Every time he switched a flavor, he would remove one tag and slide a new one in. Sometimes he changed the menu a few times in one day, such as replacing "Double-Bold" with "Low-Jitter" after noon.

MegaCup took a different approach. The manager quickly found that, while adding new shingles to the end of the list was easy, removing them was frustrating. In order to remove a shingle, he had to: unlink it from both the shingle above and the shingle below, then reattach the shingle below to the one above. It was a time-consuming process. He decided to take advantage of the sign's ability to easily expand offerings. He instead offered six different coffees on a semi-permanent basis. On rare occasions, he would grudgingly spend fifteen minutes unlinking a shingle on his sign and adding a new one.

The two coffee shops operated in that mode for years. Zed's coffee shop rotated through different options, and MegaCup offered a more constant, but larger, selection.

Both businesses thrived as the market for coffee grew. Eventually, Zed's Coffee House became one of the largest businesses in the kingdom, with over a hundred different locations. Zed continued to expand aggressively until the great sugar famine hit. With business dropping due to the lack of sugar, Zed decided to leave the world of coffee and speculate in coconut sales.

Strings and Pigeon Messages

Strings are sequences of characters. In many programming languages, strings are implemented as an array of characters, and you can access each character as you would any value in an array.

❦

"ONLY TWENTY LETTERS?" ASKED Ann. The limit seemed ridiculous. Who had ever heard of a pigeon-carrier message with a length limit?

"Yes," confirmed Guelph's pigeon master. "We don't have the kingdom's strongest pigeons here. We need to be careful about the weight of the messages."

"But twenty letters is so short," objected Ann.

"It's actually a twenty character limit," clarified the pigeon master. "Spaces count toward your total. So does punctuation." He laid out a tiny rectangle of parchment on the counter. It had twenty tiny gray squares. Each square was large enough to hold a single character.

"I suppose we could send for a stronger pigeon," offered the pigeon master. "It might take a while, but we've done it before. I hear the castle has pigeons that can carry multiple pages of information. Can you imagine that?" He smiled wistfully and looked out the window. Ann had never seen a case of pigeon envy this bad.

Ann shrugged. Truthfully, twenty characters would be more than enough. She had yet to find any useful information about the darkness. This message was a courtesy to her father; she had promised regular updates.

Without a good reason to argue for a longer message, Ann set about filling in the tiny squares: "No progress. -Ann." Seventeen letters.

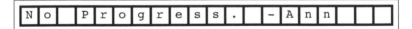

Ann took a moment to consider where she could add more information. She could strip out the punctuation, but that would save her only two characters. Anyway, she had nothing more to say.

She paid the pigeon master and watched him attach the message to the pigeon's leg. The bird lethargically flapped away, barely clearing the windowsill. Ann briefly wished that she could follow the pathetic bird back to the castle. Instead, she left the communications office and continued on her quest.

As prescribed by Sir Galwin's algorithm, Ann needed to find more information. She had no leads and her recent attempts to consult Dr. Conjunctione, Dr. Whileton, and now Dr. Iterator had failed miserably. In fact, none of the scholars she had visited could provide any assistance. They had all been too busy with "vital problems" to even speak with her. She needed some clue—any clue. So, despite her deep misgivings, she resolved to consult the Oracle of New Atlantis.

The Swimmy Friends Pet Store

Swapping two values in an array is a basic operation that helps illustrate how arrays store data. Each entry in an array can be viewed as an individual variable—it stores one piece of information. In order to swap the values contained in two different entries, additional (temporary) storage must be used. Specifically: 1) the data from one array entry is written to the temporary storage, 2) the data from the other array entry is written to the memory location of the first entry, and 3) the data from temporary storage is written to the second array entry.

※※※

C ASEY'S FIRST DAY AT the Swimmy Friends Pet Store hadn't gone smoothly. Within fifteen minutes, he had accidentally allowed all thirty turtles to escape. He had then spent the next eight hours rounding them up. Although the turtles were slow, they scattered in different directions and hid under store shelves. No matter how nicely he asked, the turtles refused to come when he called them.

The day had concluded with a stern lecture from the manager. The manager reminded Casey that Swimmy Friends Pet Store had a reputation to maintain. It was, after all, the kingdom's finest aquatic pet store. Even the king had purchased his pet turtle at Swimmy Friends, and the king's gardener had purchased a large rock here just last week.

Casey sincerely hoped that his second day would go better.

"Casey, I have a job for you," called the manager as Casey

entered the store.

"Sure!" responded Casey eagerly.

"We're starting a promotion on tiger barbs this week," the manager explained. "I want to put them in the big tank at the front of the wall. Can you swap them with the neon tetras?"

Casey looked at the fish section. Large, torch-lit fish tanks lined the entire back wall of the store. At the front was the tank currently occupied by the neon tetras. Five tanks over, two dozen tiger barbs swam lazily around a small rock. Both tanks looked quite heavy.

"You want me to move the tanks?" asked Casey.

"Of course not!" the manager answered. "The tanks are full of water and weigh more than you. Just swap the fish. The temperature and pH are already identical."

Casey nodded. He walked over to the tiger barb tank and began trying to scoop up barbs in the net. The manager watched from the side.

"What are you doing?" the manager asked.

"Moving the tiger barbs over," responded Casey without looking up. The tiger barbs were fast, and Casey wasn't coordinated. He thrashed about with his little green net, hoping that he could catch one by luck.

"You do know that tiger barbs and tetras can't go in the same tank, right?"

"Uh-huh," responded Casey, still lost in concentration.

"So, what are you going to do with the tiger barb that you're having trouble catching?" prompted the manager.

"I'm going to put it—oh." Casey realized his mistake. There was no way he could transfer the tiger barbs over without first moving the tetras. And there was no way to transfer the tetras over without first moving the tiger barbs. The whole swap was deadlocked. His brain spun as he tried to come up with a solution.

The manager waited for Casey to see the solution. It wasn't a hard problem. Finally, after two minutes, the manager realized that Casey wasn't going to figure it out.

"Use that empty tank as temporary storage," the manager prompted. "First, put the tetras in the empty tank. Second, move the tiger barbs to the old tetra tank. Third, move the tetras to the old tiger barb tank."

"But that means three sets of moving things. I know that I can do it in two." Casey responded. He was determined to prove that he was a good employee.

The manager sighed. "No. You can't. You need to use temporary storage. Otherwise, you'll end up putting tiger barbs in the tetra tank and causing problems."

Casey wanted to argue, but he couldn't think of a better solution. "Okay," he finally agreed.

The manager looked at Casey. While he was semi-confident that Casey could handle the fish swap, he worried about Casey doing something stupid later.

"Come find me when you finish," the manager instructed. "And stay away from the turtle tank," he added for good measure.

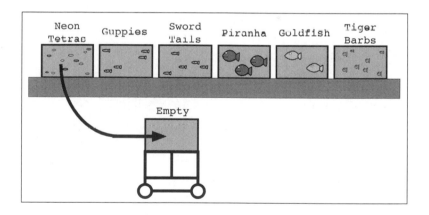

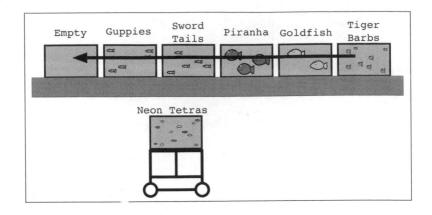

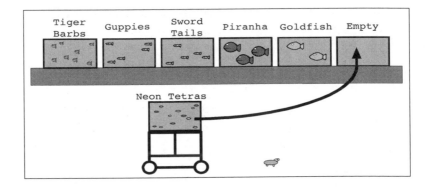

Pointers and Walk-In Closets

Pointers are variables that hold a particular type of data: addresses in the computer's memory. A main advantage of using pointers is the flexibility that they provide when interacting with data stored in memory. A single, relatively small pointer can give the location of a massive chunk of data sitting in memory, allowing functions to access the data without passing around the full block of data itself. Programmers can also create complex data structures by using pointers to link blocks of data.

❧

THE POWERFUL WIZARD MARCUS lived in a small townhouse in downtown New Athens. It had high rent and terrible views, but that was the price of living downtown. To be honest, neither of those factors bothered Marcus. What annoyed him was the the townhouse's size. Marcus had accumulated many belongings over the years, and he liked having a place to store them. The townhouse had only one closet, and it was pathetically small.

Being a powerful magician, Marcus turned to magical solutions to improve the situation. First, he shrunk his belongings so everything fit in his closet. However, he could never find anything in the resulting heap of tiny items. One night he spent two hours on the floor with a magnifying glass, searching for his favorite wizard's hat. As a result, he arrived tremendously late for a date.

Next, he tried dehydrating his possessions to powder and putting them in labeled jars. His closet soon resembled a spice rack.

Unfortunately, rehydrating clothes left them thoroughly soaked, and a single poorly timed sneeze scattered his favorite cloak over his living room. Marcus quickly abandoned that idea as well.

Finally, he came to a stunning realization. He didn't need to keep all of his possessions right here. As long as he could easily retrieve them when needed, he could store them anywhere.

He bought a huge castle in the rural outlands to store his belongings. When he needed an object, he would summon it. Similarly, when he finished with it, he would send it back. The process effectively gave him a giant virtual closet.

In only a short matter of time, Marcus found that he had a new problem. He no longer remembered what was in the castle or even how much space he had left. Fashions from previous years lay forgotten throughout the castle's halls. He found himself randomly summoning items from different rooms in the castle just to see what was there—a process that led to the disturbing discovery of a two-year-old blueberry muffin. Marcus needed a better system.

In order to keep track of the items he had stored in the castle and their locations, Marcus created a formal accounting system. He divided the castle into a giant, labeled grid of squares. Then he created a scroll listing all of his items. Each time he sent an item to the castle, he carefully recorded a pointer to where he had sent that object. Using this scroll, he could find the location from which to summon any item. He needed to keep only one small scroll of pointers in his downtown townhouse. This system worked well.

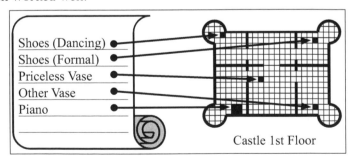

Shoes (Dancing)
Shoes (Formal)
Priceless Vase
Other Vase
Piano

Castle 1st Floor

Or, at least, the system worked well most of the time. Occasionally, Marcus got careless and forgot to record where he sent an item. As a result the item was lost and the space inside the castle wasted. Other times, Marcus would forget to check that a space was free before sending an object there. One night, after returning from a party, he accidentally sent his coat to the same location as a priceless vase. The vase exploded as the large coat appeared inside it. These were the inherent dangers of carelessness with his pointers.

Despite the occasional accident, the system worked well. Marcus learned to be careful about tracking everything in his scroll, and he lived happily in his small townhouse in the most fashionable neighborhood in New Athens.

Linked Lists and Ocean Voyages

Linked lists are data structures that store lists of items. Each node in the list consists of a few pieces of data: the information being stored at that node (or a pointer to it), a pointer to the next node in the list, and (optionally) a pointer to the previous node in the list. An algorithm can traverse the items in a list by simply following the pointer out of each node to the next. Linked lists allow the user to insert and remove elements easily, simply by changing the appropriate nodes' pointers.

ANN HAD BEEN EXCITED about her ocean voyage to visit the Oracle of New Atlantis for approximately twenty minutes. She had stood at the ship's railing, watching the shoreline move away and feeling the sea breeze on her face. The ship's sails had made a pleasant flapping noise as they caught the wind. It had been exhilarating. Then, much to her dismay, the ship had started a nauseating series of sways and lurches.

Bundled up against the (now remarkably frigid) breeze, Ann sat on the ship's deck and watched the three ships following silently after them. The first trailed four hundred meters behind, the second four hundred meters after that, and the third another four hundred meters behind. In addition, Ann knew that another ship led the way, four hundred meters in front of them. Together the five ships made a convoy that stretched out in a mile-long line across the ocean.

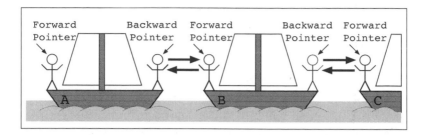

Ann had found the arrangement of the convoy fascinating. When she had interrogated the captain as to the convoy's linear arrangement, he had happily explained the line's functionality in exquisite detail. The convoy consisted of a chain of ships navigating along the same route. The head ship led the convoy. This arrangement facilitated both navigation and safety.

Communication among the ships also fascinated Ann. Each ship had two special crew members, called *pointers*, who handled communication with the other ships. The pointer in the rear of one ship could communicate with the pointer at the front of following ship by using large, brightly colored flags. Sadly, it had taken a comment from the captain before Ann realized that the pointers were passing messages. It had honestly looked as though they were simply being friendly and, perhaps, a bit too enthusiastic.

When ship #2 wanted to pass a message to ship #5, the pointer at the back of ship #2 would signal the message to the pointer at the front of ship #3. Similarly, through pointers, ship #3 would relay it to ship #4 and ship #4 to ship #5. It was a completely linear system, with the message passing through each ship on its way.

The whole arrangement reminded Ann of her days as a young kindergartener when the students would be forced to hold hands as they went on field trips. Each kid would maintain contact with exactly two classmates, ensuring that the full string of students stayed completely connected. The teachers would walk down the line, carefully comparing the students to a list of names.

But in Ann's mind, the best thing about the kindergarten lines was their ability to be dynamic. In the event that Ann had to visit the restroom, she would leave the line by simply making sure that the students on either side of her held hands with each other. When she returned, she would pick a point to insert herself in the line, break the line at that point, and reform the connections by holding hands with her new neighbors. Since all such new arrivals often forgot to dry their hands, the process also included loud complaints from the new neighbors. These kindergarten lines had opened Ann's eyes to the power of dynamic data structures.

"Captain, do your convoys ever get additions or removals?" Ann asked one morning. "Or is the convoy fixed once it departs?"

"Of course the convoy changes," the captain answered. "In fact, later today we have three ships joining us from North Patagonia." He gestured vaguely toward the direction of North Patagonia as if to illustrate his point.

"Will they join the end of the line?" asked Ann, eager to understand the convoy's dynamics. It would make sense to simply append the new ships to the end of the line. That way only the first ship of the new arrivals and the last ship of the current convoy would need to connect. That's how they had merged lines in kindergarten.

"No, no," insisted the captain. "They'll join between ships #4 and #5. Ship #5 is a special warship with extra rear-facing cannons. It has to be in the back. One by one the ships will insert themselves into the chain, coordinating through their pointers. Good sailors, those pointers."

"But how?" asked Ann.

"All very simply, I assure you. The new ship, let's call it D, will pull up next to our head ship and then slow down. It will slowly work its way down the convoy until it finds a location to insert itself: let's say between ship A and ship B. Then the pointers are reassigned. D's backward pointer now talks to B. B's forward pointer now talks to D. A's backward pointer now talks to D. And D's forward pointer now talks to A. It's all very organized."

Ann was thrilled. When the ships arrived that afternoon, she watched their coordinated dance with glee. The simplicity of it amazed her. Inserting a new ship into the line was only a matter of reassigning four pointers, two in each direction. In her excitement over the dynamic operations of the convoy, Ann even managed to forget about her seasickness.

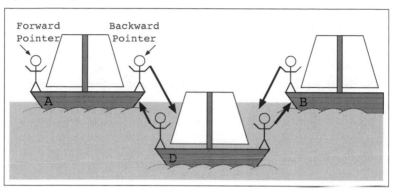

The Prince's Complaint Line

Stacks, queues, and priority queues are data structures that control the order in which data is extracted. Stacks are last-in, first-out data structures that return the most recent data inserted. Queues are first-in, first-out data structures that return the least recent data inserted. Priority queues return the highest priority data inserted (accord to some priority value).

❧

B EFORE HE BECAME KING, Prince Fredrick had a tradition of hearing his future subjects' complaints every Tuesday in the Great Room. At 10 a.m. the doors would open and his loyal subjects would fill the room to raise their complaints. On the days he felt particularly generous, Prince Fredrick would even task his steward with addressing some of the complaints. However, on most days, Fredrick believed that he had done his part just by listening to them.

By 6 a.m. every Tuesday, a large crowd would form outside the doors to the Hall of Complaints. Farmers with particularly pressing concerns camped out for days or weeks, hoping to be near the front of the crowd and thus be selected to discuss their complaint. The fact that their complaint would likely be ignored did not dampen their resolve. They needed to be heard.

Fredrick never gave much thought to what happened before the doors opened. After all, he was the prince. Why should he care about what happened outside of his room?

Then, Rok the Dragon arrived. In early June the dragon started burning crop fields and eating the livestock—typical dragon activities. However, Fredrick continued to use his system, selecting the subjects from the front of the room.

In late July, Fredrick finally selected a farmer who was there to talk about the dragon. "What is your complaint?" asked Fredrick.

"A dragon ate my farm," the farmer answered.

"A dragon?" Fredrick repeated. "We must act now before it destroys a second farm!"

Silence followed Prince Fredrick's proclamation.

"What is it?" Fredrick asked, but nobody responded. Fredrick singled out another farmer and directed the question at him.

"It's just—well—the dragon has destroyed over twenty farms since it arrived here in June. My farm was destroyed six weeks ago."

"Why am I only hearing about it now?" yelled the prince.

"Noble sir, I've been lining up for six weeks to discuss the dragon. It's only today that you gave me an audience."

"How many others are here to talk about the dragon?" inquired the prince. Half the people in the room raised their hands. The prince screamed at everyone in general. Eventually, he calmed down enough to send knights to run the dragon out of town.

"This will never happen again," the prince vowed. "Henceforth there will be a *system*. Each person will write down his or her complaint and put it on top of a complaint stack. Each Tuesday from 10 a.m. to 11 a.m. I will take the top complaints off the stack and read them. This way I will always hear the most recent complaints."

Everyone in the room looked at each other. They gave a half-hearted cheer: "Yay."

For the next few months life returned to normal and the Royal Complaint Stack worked about as well as the unorganized mob of people in the complaint room. Then Rok returned. On Wednesday, he ate one farm and took a week-long nap.

On the following Tuesday, the prince read through the first

ten complaints on the stack. All ten were about the refereeing at last Sunday's sporting event. The blue team had lost and, as is typical, its fans were unhappy with the referees. The prince had an easy solution; he told the steward to bet against the blue team next week. Feeling like he had fulfilled his duty to the people, the prince decided to quit early and play some golf.

The prince screamed when he found the dragon sleeping on the golf course. "What is it doing here? Why was I not told?" He threw his golf clubs at his caddy in frustration and stormed back to the castle.

He was still fuming when he got back to the Great Room. "I should have been told. Why did no one complain?"

"Your honor," started the steward carefully. Fredrick picked up on his tone immediately.

"Where is the complaint stack?" he demanded. The steward brought in the stack of complaint papers. The prince leafed through them. The top eight were something about food poisoning from today's special at some local restaurant. Under those were more complaints about refereeing. Then he found it. Complaint number thirty-one on the stack mentioned the dragon.

"Curses!" he yelled at the stack of papers.

"No more complaining about minor things when there are important problems!" the prince declared.

The steward sighed. "Sir, how will we tell? The people want to be able to complain about what's bothering them."

"Then there shall be a *new system*!"

Everyone groaned quietly.

The prince retired to his study and began working on the new system. It had to let people voice their frustrations. It had to allow the prince to find the most important issues. More importantly, it couldn't take too much of his time; he really hated dealing with complaints. He spent three weeks in isolation working on his system.

The following Monday, he addressed his subjects. "I have devised a new system that uses a priority queue. Each of you shall write your complaints on a piece of paper. Every Monday night, the steward shall read each complaint and assign a priority from 0 to 10. We shall then deal with the highest priority complaints first." The prince paused and waited for the applause. A few subjects clapped in a lackluster fashion. The steward audibly groaned at his new task. He knew quite well that everyone would complain to him about the assigned priorities.

Thus the kingdom adopted a priority-based complaint system. Over time, the subjects embraced this system. The prince went on to become king and guide his kingdom through a period of unprecedented happiness and quick responses to dragons. Everyone in the kingdom was happy—except, of course, the steward.

Binary Search Trees and the Spider

Binary search trees (BST) organize data to allow efficient searches by value. Data is stored in tree nodes. Each tree node also maintains pointers to at most two child nodes: a left child and right child. The tree maintains the property that, at each node, values down the left child are less than the value of the current node. In contrast, values down the right child are greater than (or equal to) the value in the current node. This structure allows you to search efficiently by walking down the tree and branching in the direction of the value for which you are looking.

❧

S PECK LIVED A TYPICAL spider lifestyle. He built webs, ate flies, and enjoyed discussing the weather with his neighbors. In fact, for those who had never been to visit his web, he seemed like a perfectly normal spider.

However, Speck had a most unusual quirk for a spider. He was obsessive about his food choices and demanded a level of variety that was unheard-of among arachnids. Speck insisted on keeping a supply of at least 25 different types of bugs in his web.

Speck also insisted on absolute organization in his food supply. What good were 25 varieties of bugs if he couldn't quickly find the one he wanted? While most spiders kept their bugs distributed randomly throughout their webs, that prospect seemed absurd to Speck. He loathed such disorganization. Instead, like any rational chef, Speck organized his food choices in alphabetical order.

The result of these preferences was a new type of web, which Speck developed through days of trial and error. He called it a binary search web. He firmly believed that it would revolutionize the world of bug storage.

The web consisted of nodes—clusters of webbing storing his bugs—and strings of web between the nodes. The whole web was organized vertically. At the top, a single "root" node hung from a wooden beam. Each node could have at most two "child" nodes below it. These nodes were attached securely to their parent node using a strong strand of webbing. As a result, the web branched out wider as it progressed downwards, taking on a vaguely triangular shape.

In order to organize his bugs, Speck used the nodes to enforce a particular alphabetical ordering. If you were standing on any node in the web, then all of the bugs down the left-hand path had to be before the current node's bug in alphabetical order. Similarly, all of the bugs down the right-hand path had to be after the current node's bug in alphabetical order. So if you wanted to find a particular bug, you could always use the current node's bug to choose whether to go left or right.

For example, one morning Speck decided that he wanted a fly for breakfast. He started at the top of his web, where he slept, and examined the bug there. It was a ladybug. Although it wasn't the bug he wanted, it told him which way to go. Since flies come before ladybugs alphabetically, Speck chose the left child node to continue his search.

At the next node, Speck found a beetle. His stomach turned at the sight of it. Admittedly, Speck had never been too fond of beetles, and the thought of one for breakfast was deeply unpleasant. He hurried past that node. This time he knew to go right, because flies come after beetles.

Thus, Speck found the three day old fly. He happily ate his breakfast and then took a mid-morning nap.

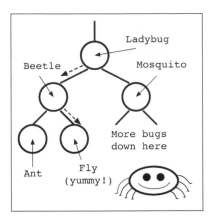

Since Speck got cranky whenever he was hungry, he found the efficiency provided by the web critical. The web's branching structure often allowed Speck to find any bug in just a short walk. In fact, Speck could double his inventory of bugs by adding just one new level to his web.

The web also lent itself to the addition and removal of bugs. Adding a new bug simply consisted of walking the bug down the web (while taking the correct alphabetical branches) until he hit a dead end. Then he would add a new child node, with the new bug, to the correct side of the current node. Adding a new node meant spinning some webs, and Speck enjoyed that part of being a spider. As he saw it, making webs was definitely the best part of being a spider.

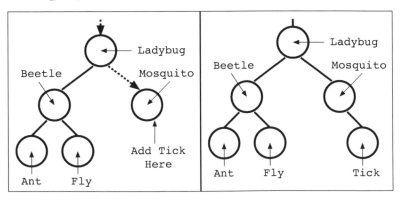

When Speck finished with a bug, he would simply remove it from the web. If there were two nodes below the now-empty node, he would move a bug up to fill the empty spot. He was always careful to do this in such a way as to maintain the tree's structure and sorted property. If there was only one child node, he would shift that child node into the place of the empty node. At the end, he would be left with a single empty node that he could cut out of the tree and let drift off in the wind.

Sadly, despite the obvious advantages of the binary web structure, Speck never managed to encourage wide adoption. His friends stuck with the classic circular patterns and continued to eat whichever bugs were closest.

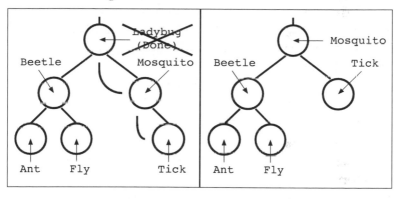

Pointers, Linked Lists, and Trees

Pointers can be used to link together blocks of data and create complex data structures. For example, each node in a linked list may contain a pointer to the next node. This node may live in a completely different area of the computer's memory, but the pointer allows the program to move from one node to the next. Similarly, the nodes in a binary tree contain pointers to their child nodes.

❧

"**D**O YOU WANT ME to squish it?" the ship's captain asked loudly.

Ann jumped and turned in surprise. With a rising sense of embarrassment, she realized that she had been staring at the spider's web for the last two hours. In that time, the galley had emptied and the crew had returned to work.

"No," Ann answered hastily. "It's fascinating."

"Fascinating?" asked the captain. "It's a spider. How interesting can it be?"

Ann turned back to the web. "I've never seen a web like this before; it ..." Ann's voice drifted off as she struggled to describe the web. "It looks like a binary search tree," she continued. "See how the tiny nodes of web are joined together by thin linkages, and how each node has at most two child nodes."

"Binary search tree?" asked the captain. "It is an oddly shaped web, to be sure. But I don't see how it looks like a tree."

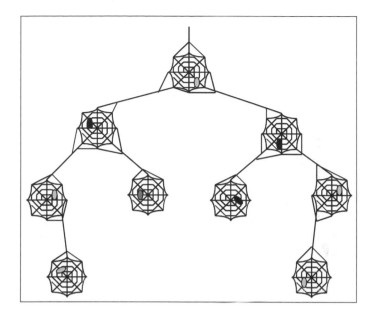

Ann thought for a moment to draw a comparison that the captain would understand. "Your convoy!" she exclaimed suddenly. "It's like your convoy."

The captain leaned in. "It looks nothing like my convoy. My convoy is a straight line. This web branches out in weird ways. Moreover, this web has bugs! Lots of bugs. I think there's even a beetle in there."

"Think about pointers," Ann interrupted. "In the convoy each ship is a node—a self-contained unit bearing some cargo. The ships are joined together into a line by pointers. A pointer links each ship to the one behind it, like a giant linked list."

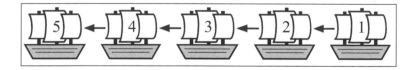

"The web is similar," Ann continued. "Each node seems to have a 'cargo' of a single bug. The threads of web joining them together are like pointers."

"Why not make it a line?" asked the captain. "Why does it branch out like that?"

"I have no idea what this particular spider is trying to do or why he built this web like this," answered Ann. "But, in the case of binary search trees, the branching structure makes searching for a specific node very fast."

"You think this spider is organizing his bugs?"

"Of course not," answered Ann. "Or…probably not. But the similarity is remarkable."

Both Ann and the captain stood in silence, watching the spider disconnect an empty node at the bottom of his web. The empty webbing floated away in the breeze.

"Like a ship leaving the convoy," Ann noted, marveling at how the web's nodes were linked together.

"Do you think we should put our ships into one of these 'trees'?" the captain asked.

"Why would you do that?" asked Ann.

"Well…you make it sound like a superior way of organizing things," said the captain.

Ann shrugged. "Different data structures are meant for different things. Binary search trees are good for searching. Linked lists are good for storing a sequence of data.

"I think that a line works better in your case," she continued. "If you used a tree, the convoy would branch out as it went back—each ship would have two ships linked behind it. It would be terribly difficult to navigate into the harbor. I'm sure at least one ship would run aground. And you would likely confuse every fishing boat in your path."

Ann shook her head at the image of a giant tree of ships bearing down on a small fishing boat. "No," she concluded. "It wouldn't work well at all."

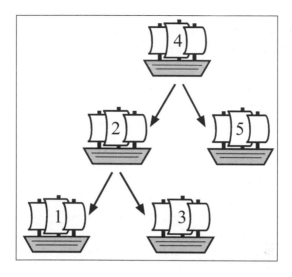

The captain nodded and looked relieved. Ann wondered if he had actually been willing to reconsider the convoy's formation based on a few offhand comments about a spider's web. However, she let the matter drop so as not to embarrass the captain. After exchanging a few more pleasantries with her, the captain returned to his duties.

Ann continued to watch the spider for another two hours, fascinated by the web's strange design and the unknown reasons behind it.

Caching and the Library of Alexandria

Caching data means storing a copy of the data in a quickly accessible location to speed up future accesses of that data. The key trade-off is that the faster storage locations for data tend to be smaller and thus hold less data. For example, accessing data from RAM is much faster than reading it off a hard drive, but RAM is both smaller and more expensive per unit of storage. By caching data that is used often, you can greatly speed up a program.

THE LIBRARY OF ALEXANDRIA is still famous to this day for the size and breadth of its collection. However, few people know that the true magic of the library was the librarian's ability to find relevant resources with amazing speed. Within a few seconds he could often locate the canonical reference to answer a patron's question.

For young Peter, this magical ability had always been a thing of wonder. He had grown up in a small house four blocks from the library and had spent many afternoons sitting at the tables listening to the librarian answer questions:

"What should I feed my new pet yak?"

"Where can I find the sweetest prunes in Alexandria?"

The scope of knowledge commanded by the librarian was almost legendary. Peter dreamed of one day learning the magic. And, after ten years of training, Peter got his wish: he was accepted as the librarian's apprentice.

On the first day of his apprenticeship, Peter arrived three hours early. As the librarian took him on a tour of the library, Peter eagerly followed him around, scribbling notes into his new notebook. Although Peter knew the public areas by heart, he soaked in every word. After the tour was complete, the librarian and his new apprentice took their places behind the reference desk and waited for the first patron of the day.

The first question came from a small man holding a rather large rock. "I'm trying to build a wheel. And, well ... I'm not sure what shape to go with. Do you have any good references?"

The librarian disappeared into the stacks, only to reappear a few seconds later with a scroll entitled "Wheels and How to Design Them." The patron was delighted. He took the scroll over to a nearby desk and started to quickly skim through it.

"Oh ... I see ... a circle ... hmm ... brilliant," the patron quietly mumbled to himself.

"How did you do that?" The apprentice asked. "How did you find the scroll so quickly? Please teach me the magic of the library."

"Magic?" The librarian asked. "I'm not sure about that, but I can show you my system."

The librarian led Peter into the back room. The room was dimly lit by two small oil lamps. At the back was a single door leading to the vaults where the thousands of scrolls were kept. The librarian walked over to the a small table that held a coffee pot and a small stack of scrolls. He pointed at the scrolls. "I usually find the answers in one of these."

Peter was confused. "Twenty scrolls? The library has tens of thousands of scrolls. How does having twenty in the back room help? Are they magic?"

"Not at all," chuckled the librarian. "It turns out that people are pretty boring. They all ask the same types of questions. In fact, I've found that 95% of the questions in a single day can be answered with only twenty scrolls."

"Is that all?" Peter asked, visibly disappointed.

"Yes," replied the librarian. "What did you hope for?"

"I'm not sure. But I was certainly expecting something magical. Maybe you were summoning the scrolls or could teleport yourself to the correct shelf. But ... this seems like cheating."

"Cheating?" The librarian laughed. "Do you realize how much effort goes into making this efficient enough to appear magical? You can't pick *any* twenty scrolls. They have to be the *right* twenty scrolls."

At the news of this challenge, the apprentice perked up a bit. "And how do you pick them? Telepathy?"

"When I first started, I kept the most frequently read scrolls in my cache. Every time someone read a scroll, I would note that. I kept a count for each scroll."

"I see why that would work," said the apprentice, sounding slightly bored.

"Aha! But it *didn't* work!" exclaimed the librarian. "Everything seemed to be going fine, until the same scrolls got stuck in my cache. Remember that massive flood we had two years ago? During the entire flood, I still had three scrolls on how to survive a drought. It was a disaster."

"Then I had a new idea," he continued. "I could keep more data and use statistics. I meticulously kept track of which scrolls people were viewing and correlated it to the season, weather, and fads of the day. I created complex predictive models of which scrolls would be most requested on a given day. I could pre-fill my shelf every morning!"

"Did that work?" asked Peter.

"Yes. But was a lot of work. So I stopped doing it."

Peter stared at the floor. Disappointment flowed through him. He wondered if he should have become a blacksmith instead.

"Eventually, I got lazy and left the most recent scrolls on the shelf. When I needed to go down to the stacks, I'd grab whatever scroll had been used least recently and put it back. It turned out to be a pretty good system."

"Really? So the magic behind the Library of Alexandria is that you keep the twenty most recently viewed scrolls on a shelf in the back room?"

"Yes. It allows me to answer 95% of people's questions without going past this room."

The apprentice nodded numbly. Now he was certain that he should have become a blacksmith.

Algorithms

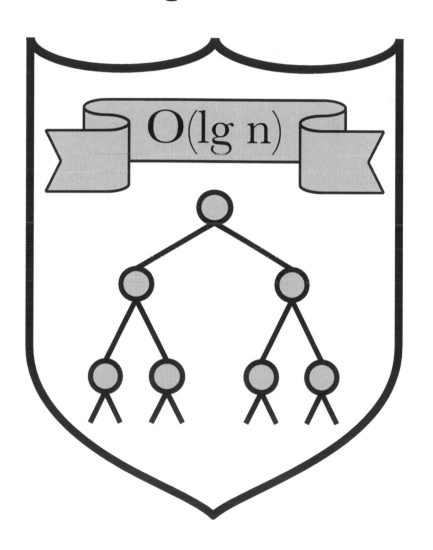

Functions and Sailing

Functions are self-contained blocks of code within a program. They have defined inputs and outputs, and they can be called from other parts of the code. Functions allow programmers to reuse a common block of code in different places within the program.

❧

AFTER WITNESSING THE SHIP'S pointers in action, Ann became fascinated by all aspects of the ship's operations. She spent hours observing the ship's crew. Ann watched as the sailors hoisted sails, tied off ropes, cleaned the decks, and recorded headings. She marveled at the flawless skills of the seasoned sailors and at the stubborn clumsiness of a cook's assistant. Driven by intense curiosity, Ann tried to learn as much as possible about each job.

One morning, Ann even asked the caption if she could borrow a copy of the ship's manual. Always eager to help, the captain soon returned with a 4,096-page *Sailor's Manual (3rd edition)*. Ann was shocked.

"Why is it so large?" she asked.

"There's a lot to know," responded the captain with pride. "It takes the average sailor five years to learn the basics and another thirty-five to learn the rest of the manual."

"I see," Ann said. A forty-year education seemed rather excessive. Then again, it probably took years to simply read through the manual itself. In Ann's experience, operational manuals were rarely quick reads.

After thanking the captain, Ann took the manual to a quiet, shady corner. She flipped through, glancing at the different subjects. She skimmed past the many pages devoted to regulation beard lengths and the care of parrots. Finally, she selected the topic of securing the ship to the dock. The instructions occupied three full pages of tiny print. The level of detail astounded Ann. Each instruction spelled out every last aspect of the task.

Ann read each line, trying to absorb the information. She even practiced the instructions for tying the ropes into knots (twenty-five lines long) on her own shoe laces, and then promptly berated herself for not recognizing the common granny knot. After about half an hour, she felt confident in her understanding of the procedure.

The following section described how to secure a dinghy to the ship. Again, the section occupied three pages of tiny print. As Ann skimmed the pages, she began to recognize instructions from the last section. In fact, the twenty-five lines about tying the rope were absolutely identical. She flipped back and forth rapidly between the two sections to confirm.

The next day, Ann approached the captain about this discovery.

"How observant!" he congratulated her. "Many of the concepts are similar. For example, take ropes. There are only a few really good ways to tie knots."

"Then why repeat the instructions line for line?" asked Ann.

"You need to do them each time," answered the captain. "It would be horrible to skip the part about tying the knot. The dinghy would drift off. There was a terrible incident a few years ago with a canoe—"

"I understand that," Ann interrupted. "But you don't need to repeat everything. Why not say something like: 'Tie the rope with a granny knot'? It would save you a lot of space—24 lines in this section alone. All you need to do is to break out the common tasks into their own sets of instructions."

"That might make it much harder to understand the

instructions," said the captain. "Right now, every step is laid out perfectly. I can hand any sailor the thirty-five pages about trimming the main sail without having to assume any prior knowledge. It would surprise you how many new sailors don't read the entire manual during their first week!"

"Reusing core concepts would make the manual easier to understand," argued Ann. "Once a sailor learns how to tie a specific knot, he or she could do it in any context. It would become a fundamental step itself—like a computer function."

"I guess it would make things shorter," agreed the captain. "But really, the length of the book is not a problem. We also use the books for ballast, so having heavy books can be useful."

"It's better than that," argued Ann, ignoring the comment about ballast. "What if you found a better knot? Right now you'd have to change every single instruction that uses the current knot. It'd probably be a long and error-prone process. If you write the same thing a hundred times, you'll make a mistake one of those times. You probably have dozens of mistakes in here already."

The captain winced sightly, and Ann wondered if the suggestion of possible errors had gone too far. Criticizing a captain was always risky.

"What if you want to instruct a sailor to do something new, such as tie down a hot air balloon?" Ann continued. "Do you have instructions for that?"

"Well, no," admitted the captain. He instinctively reached for a notepad and jotted down a reminder to add a section on hot air balloons.

"It would be easier to say: 1) Grab the rope, and 2) Tie it to the port railing with a granny knot. Those are instructions you can even give verbally. The sailor only needs to know how to perform a few basic functions to start."

The captain fell silent and stared out into the sea. After a moment he nodded slowly.

"I think you're right!" he declared loudly. After a few days at sea with him, Ann had realized that the captain was a big fan of declaring things loudly. More importantly, he was also open to improving processes whenever possible.

Ann smiled.

"I bet it goes beyond simply tying ropes. The signals we use to communicate can be broken off into functions too. And all of the lamps are refilled with the same procedure. And the decks are all mopped in the same way—counterclockwise mopping, of course. And there's beard trimming..." The captain trailed off as he slowly looked around the ship, assessing the reuse of different skills.

Suddenly, he spun back toward Ann. "Will you help me rewrite the book? We could break things up into these stand-alone units you describe. It would revolutionize the entire sailing industry!"

Ann's smile faltered. While the opportunity to improve the performance of the entire royal navy was tempting, her quest came first. If she didn't save the kingdom, there would be no navy at all. So, with much regret, she declined the offer. Instead, she agreed to write her father and request that six of the kingdom's top computational thinkers aid the effort. Satisfied that together they would be as helpful as herself, Ann let her mind wander to other questions.

Big-O Notation and the Wizards' War

Big-O notation is a method of specifying the worst-case performance of an algorithm as the size of the problem grows. Big-O notation is important for understanding how algorithms scale and for comparing the relative performance of two algorithms.

❧❧❧

Y EARS AGO, A FEROCIOUS wizards' war raged across the land. Initially sparked by a disagreement over the correct pronunciation of the word "elementary," the conflict quickly escalated. The battles lasted months. Neither side could gain an upper hand. The strength of the two sides was almost perfectly matched—until a computational theorist shifted the balance of power forever.

Clare O'Connell was not a wizard, but rather an accountant. She worked in the Bureau of Farm Animal Accounting: Large Mammal Division, where she spent her days tracking the kingdom's cows, horses, sheep, and pigs. It wasn't an exciting job, but it left her plenty of time to pursue other interests, such as computational theory. In fact, in only three years after her arrival, Clare had assembled the kingdom's greatest collection of computational theorists within the bureau.

Clare had never taken any notice of the war until she was caught in the middle of a battle. Wizards' wars tended to be well separated from daily civilian life. The wizards would bicker and fight amongst themselves, but would rarely resort to any spell that had an impact on the general population. In fact, they avoided spells that could cause any actual physical harm altogether.

During one early May morning, Clare was accidentally caught in the crossfire. She had been leaving the baker's shop when a stray spell turned her bread into a frog. The true target, a loaf of pumpernickel held by the wizard behind her, remained unscathed and quite edible. Unfortunately, the same could not be said for Clare's bread, which promptly hopped out of her hand and down the street. Clare was furious.

That morning, Clare resolved to break the stalemate and end the war for good. Since she didn't have a strong opinion on the pronunciation of "elementary," she chose to meet with the commander of the closest faction. During a three-hour meeting, she grilled him about the war's progress. In the process, she learned how wizards thought about their spells. The interview ended with one unmistakable conclusion: wizards knew nothing about computational complexity. Years of casting spells had made them lazy and inefficient.

Clare knew that the first side to relearn the importance of computational complexity would win the war. So, she called together all of the wizards from the closest faction for a tutorial at the local pub.

"Your problem is that your techniques are inefficient," she began.

The wizards mumbled in protest. How dare this accountant lecture them on the art of casting spells? They threatened to transform her drink, a well-made and perfectly heated mug of tea, into oatmeal.

"But there's a solution!" Clare continued. "There's a new technique, called Big-O notation, that will shift the tides. This notation tells you how a spell performs as the size of the battle increases, allowing you to know which spell is most efficient. You simply ask: how many steps does it take to cast a spell when facing N different enemies? Then you strip out all the constant factors and focus on just the parts that grow the fastest."

"For example," Clare continued, "if a spell takes three steps to cast, regardless of the number of enemies, then it's an $O(1)$ spell—constant cost. In contrast, if you need a single step for each pair of enemies then the cost is $O(N^2)$—quadratic cost. In a large battle, you want spells that will scale well."

The wizards grumbled in protest.

"That would never work."

"It simplifies the problem too much."

"This accountant is crazy!"

Clare was unfazed. "What's your favorite spell?" she asked a wizard in the front row.

He turned red at being singled out and mumbled, "The Spell of Pairwise Protection."

"Which does ... ?" prompted Clare.

"Well, if you cast it on an enemy and a friend, the friend is protected from that enemy for a full five minutes."

"How long does it take to cast?"

"Two seconds. It's a fast spell."

"But how well does it scale?" asked Clare.

"Scale?" asked the wizard.

"I mean: how does the performance change as you add more and more people to the battle?" explained Clare. "The performance of this spell depends on how many people are in the battle."

The wizard looked back blankly.

Clare sighed. "When you're in a large battle, you need to understand how the cost of using a spell increases as the number of people in the battle increases. Let's take the Spell of Things Smelling Like Fish. You cast it once for each enemy in the battle and they smell rotting fish for the next half an hour. One step for each enemy, so it's an $O(N)$ spell. It scales linearly with the number of enemies."

"In contrast," Clare continued, "the Spell of Pairwise Protection requires you to cast it on each pair of friends and enemies. If there are N enemies and M friends, you need to cast it $M \cdot N$

times—one step for each pair. So the cost is $O(M \cdot N)$. If you have a lot of friends, that's going to take a while."

"Good thing Henry doesn't have many friends," someone joked from the back row. A few muffled laughs followed. Clare ignored the comment.

"The Spell of Things Smelling Like Fish takes 15 seconds to cast," objected a wizard in the back row. "Your Big-O notation doesn't capture that!"

"You're right," admitted Clare. "Big-O notation is only used to compare how spells scale as the size of the battle scales. This is where your strategy is lacking. You're still accustomed to the simpler world of dueling, where the number of enemies is always one. You focus too much on the constant factors."

Clare continued, "At some size of battle, an $O(N^2)$ spell will always take much much longer than an $O(N)$ spell. At some point, the constant factors don't matter anymore. That's the value of Big-O notation."

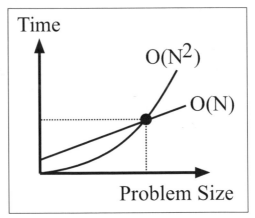

The same wizard went back on the offensive. "Are you telling me that it's better to cast the Spell of Loud Techno Music, which takes one hour and impacts all enemies, than the Spell of Temporary Elevator Music, which takes one minute but impacts only one enemy? It would seem that that is what your Big-O notation would recommend."

"Yes," said Clare. "If there are more than 60 enemies, the Spell of Loud Techno Music is more efficient the Spell of Temporary Elevator Music."

The wizard was stunned. He repeated the math over and over in his head to check her answer. Clare knew that he would eventually come to the same result. Accountants were notoriously good with numbers.

"What about the Spell of Love Triangles? That takes only one second to cast and the results are so much fun to watch," argued another wizard.

"You need to cast it on *all* triplets of people, so it's $O(N^3)$. If you have twenty opponents, that's $20 \cdot 20 \cdot 20 = 8000$ seconds! That's over two hours!"

The wizards gasped in unison. They had never thought about it like that before.

"Consider the Spell of Uncomfortably Long Toenails," suggested Clare. "This spell fell out of favor a few years ago, because it needs 120 seconds of preparation before casting it for the first time each day. It wouldn't work well in duels. However, after you perform that preparation once, it only takes five seconds per enemy. So the spell takes $120 + 5 \cdot N$ seconds for N people. Big-O notation strips out all those constant factors and simply asks, 'What happens to the cost as N gets really large?' In this case, the answer is: the Spell of Uncomfortably Long Toenails scales linearly. It's an $O(N)$ algorithm, because as N grows that's the term that dominates."

By the end of the night, Clare had convinced all of the wizards in the room to pay attention to the Big-O cost of the spells they used. It was a radical shift from the way they had always looked at their spells, focusing solely on the cost for casting it once. The Spell of Broken Command Chains, which had to be cast on all possible orderings of opponents—$O(N!)$—immediately fell out of favor. Spells that scaled well became new standards.

Tired but satisfied, Clare went home for the night. On her way home, she stopped at the baker's again for a loaf of fresh bread. While standing behind the counter, she noticed the baker using an $O(N^3)$ algorithm to make rolls. With a put-upon sigh, she interrupted the work. "You know that that isn't the most efficient way to make rolls..." she began.

Detecting Curses with Recursion

Recursion is a problem-solving technique that builds a solution to a problem from solutions to smaller subproblems of the same type. Most commonly, recursion is implemented as a function calling itself to solve the subproblems.

❧

"WHO HAS BEEN CURSED?" asked Ann. With a pang of fear, she looked around at the mob of people now surrounding her. The crowd seemed on edge.

Ann had arrived in the small coastal town of Turington minutes before the mob descended. She had planned on passing through on her journey from the docks to the city of New Atlantis itself. Then, one of the town council members had recognized her and had started pleading for her help. Within minutes, a large mob had formed. All that Ann had managed to make out was that someone was cursed.

"We don't know!" cried twenty different townsfolk. They sounded angry at the question.

"One at a time," Ann said. She quickly turned toward the town councilman. "You, and only you, tell me the problem."

"We've heard you're on a quest to save the kingdom from the darkness. It has already struck us here. One of us is cursed! You have to help us."

The last sentence sounded like a command instead of a polite request. Ann didn't like his tone. A wave of irritation flashed through her.

"A single person cursed?" asked Ann. "That doesn't sound like much of a 'coming darkness' at all."

The crowd didn't appreciate Ann's commentary. She could make out a few choice snarky comments through the general din. The people then fell into a tense silence as the town councilman spoke.

"It's a horrible curse," he said. "Can't you see that it's contagious?"

"Boils?" asked Ann. She hated curses with boils. Not only were they painful for the recipient, but they were rather unpleasant for everyone else around.

"Of course not. Do you see any boils? It's the Curse of Proximal Angst."

Instantly, the entire situation made sense to Ann. The Curse of Proximal Angst was a particularly nasty and effective curse. It used the "bad apple" theory: only one person received the curse, but it impacted everyone within a certain radius. Simply being near the cursed person caused irrational anger.

"You don't know who's cursed?" confirmed Ann. Now that she knew why she was angry, she fought to control her rage. She took a depth breath and waited for the snarky response.

The councilman also fought back his emotions. "We tried to figure it out, but to no avail. We've managed to rule out only two people: myself and Findley. Earlier today we went to get help, and the anger disappeared. Thinking that the curse had worn off, we returned. It hadn't worn off. *It is still here!*"

"Do you know the radius of the curse?" asked Ann, keeping her mind focused on business.

"At least a mile," answered the councilman.

"Can we spread everyone out that far?" asked Ann.

The councilman shook his head. "We have 512 villagers here. We can't have everyone stand at least a mile apart. There isn't room. We were thinking of sending people out one at a time, but that would take too long."

Ann thought in silence for a moment. "We'll use a recursive divide-and-conquer approach," she proclaimed.

"What's that?" asked the councilman.

"A very simple algorithm," said Ann condescendingly before she could stop herself.

"Sorry," she quickly apologized. "What I mean is that it's a simple algorithm. We start with the full town in one group. Then you split evenly into two groups—each with half the people. The two groups walk half a mile in opposite directions and wait for an hour."

"How does that help?" asked the councilman.

"At the end of the hour, only one group will be angry. That group contains the cursed individual. Once it feels better, the other group can come home."

"That only rules out half the village," protested someone in the crowd.

"True," continued Ann. "Then we recursively apply the algorithm to the remaining group. It splits in two. The two groups separate themselves, wait, and then learn which one contains the cursed individual."

The councilman nodded. "We can continue to recursively search for the cursed person. Every hour, we can eliminate half the remaining village."

"Exactly," agreed Ann. "With 512 people you'll need nine hours. First you rule out 256 people, then 128 more, then 64 more, then 32 more, then 16 more, then 8 more, then 4 more, then 2, and finally 1. You're left with the one cursed person."

"What do we do with that person?" asked the councilman.

Ann thought again. Obviously, the cursed individual needed to have the spell removed. Ann knew only one wizard she could guarantee would be able to do that. "Send him or her to a wizard that can undo the spell. The wizard Marcus lives in New Athens. He'll be able to break the spell."

Ann quickly added: "But the cursed person must find him fast. We can't have all of New Athens suffering from proximal angst.

In fact, I'd suggest running through the streets of New Athens to Marcus's door. Try yelling 'I have contagious boils!' if people won't get out of your way. Or elbow them hard as you run past."

Ann realized that she was ranting and cut herself off. The towns folk stared at her in a mixture of shock and general angst.

"Just hurry," Ann finished.

With that warning, Ann decided that it was time to leave Turington. She said a quick goodbye.

One hour and a few miles later, Ann's head began to clear. She realized that she had never asked the most basic question. Why had someone been cursed? Turington was a small town renowned for its friendly fishermen and quiet but efficient collection of flashcard authors. It was hardly the sort of place where someone would get cursed.

Ann thought briefly of going back, but she dreaded feeling the angst again. She convinced herself that it didn't matter and continued forth on her own quest.

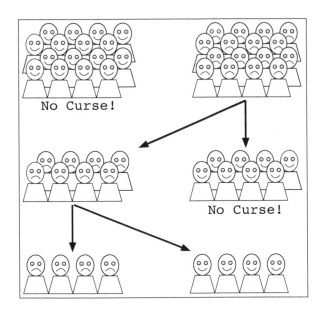

Hunting Dragons with Binary Search

Binary search is an algorithm for efficiently finding a target value within a sorted list. The algorithm maintains a shrinking search window. It narrows down that window by repeatedly ruling out half of the remaining search space. At each step, you check the middle item in the current window and compare it with the target value. If the value in the middle is less than the target value, you can rule out the lower half of the window. If the value is greater than the target value, you can rule out the upper half. This process repeats until the target item is found or the window shrinks to a single item that doesn't match the target value.

T HE MORNING'S NEWS WAS nothing short of dismal. King Fredrick had been awake for only twenty minutes when he decided that today was going to be awful. It had started manageably enough, with his head butler informing him that his favorite crown was still being polished and wasn't available. However, that news was quickly followed by a report from his acting chief knight, Sir Braver, that a dragon was now terrorizing his kingdom.

"Tell me what happened," commanded the king in a weary tone. He hated dragons.

"There's a dragon," declared Sir Braver.

"You have already told me that part. Now tell me what has *happened*. Has anyone seen this dragon? Has it attacked anyone? Has it already been here for six weeks without anyone telling me?"

prompted the king.

"We've received six confirmed sightings, sir. No one has been hurt, but Farmer McDonald has lost his prize cow. And I think it just showed up this morning, sir."

"Farmer McDonald's cow? The large one that won last year's competition?" inquired the king. If he recalled correctly, it had been a sizable cow and would have been a perfect target for the dragon.

"Yes, sir," answered the knight.

The king sighed. The story sounded like a textbook dragon attack. Soon the dragon would eat half the cows in the kingdom. "Well, you had better take the dragon hunter and vanquish the dragon."

"But sir, no one knows where the dragon is. How shall we hunt it?" asked the knight.

"Really?" the king asked, surprised that his acting head knight didn't know how to hunt a dragon. For the tenth time that week, King Fredrick regretted giving Sir Galwin a vacation.

Sir Braver remained silent.

"Find the last farm that it attacked," said the king. "Dragons take long naps after each meal, so you will have time to catch it there."

"But sir, how will we know where that is?" asked the knight.

"Have you studied dragon attacks at all?" the king asked. "There is an order to these attacks. Dragons are clever. A dragon will eat the largest cow in the area, then the second largest, then the third, and so forth. He continues to eat smaller and smaller cows until the only remaining cows are too small to be worth the bother. Then the dragon goes on to the next kingdom."

"But sir—" started the knight.

"Use the rankings from last year's cow competition!" cried the king, losing his patience. "It is a sorted list of the largest cows!"

"Ah. Of course, sir. We'll work down the list until we find the dragon!" confirmed the knight.

The king nodded, relieved that the knight was finally thinking on his own. Sir Braver and the dragon hunter would visit each of the farms on the list, in order, and find the dragon. Even as he tried to comfort himself with this thought, warning bells went off in the king's head.

"Not down the list," the king admonished. "Do you know anything about searching?"

The knight looked confused. He had been certain that he was on the correct track. "But sir, I don't understand," he said.

"How long does it take you to travel between farms?" asked the king.

"A few hours, sir."

"How many farms are on the list?"

"Maybe a hundred."

"That means it could take you hundreds of hours. By that time, the dragon will have eaten more cows. It might even have gone by then."

"But, sir—"

"Use binary search," commanded the king.

"Binary search, sir?" asked Sir Braver, regretting having fallen asleep in his Algorithms for Knights class.

"Start at the farm in the middle of the list and check whether the cow is still there. If it is still there, tear the list in half, throw away the bottom half, and repeat the process on the top half of the list. If, on the other hand, the middle cow is gone, tear the list in half, throw away the top half, and repeat the process on the bottom half of the list. Each time you visit a farm, tear the list in half and concentrate your search on only one of the two halves."

"But sir, that sounds complex," protested Sir Braver.

"It is not," argued the king. "It is simple. If the cow in the middle of the list is still at its farm, then so are all the cows below it on the list. That is how dragons eat. It will not eat a smaller cow first. That would be absurd.

"On the other hand, if the middle cow is missing, then so are all the cows above it on the list. Dragons do not eat cows randomly. There is an order to these things."

"What if the dragon moves while we search?" asked the knight.

Finally, a reasonable question. "Your search effectively tracks two bounds: the smallest cow that you know *has* been eaten and the largest cow that you know has *not* been eaten. If you get to a point where those bounds are next to each other on the list, and you do not see a dragon, then proceed to the largest uneaten cow and wait there."

"But sir, how is that any faster than simply scanning down the list?" asked the knight.

The king sighed again. His confidence in the knight's ability to handle this task was eroding rapidly. "If the dragon has attacked 45 farms, how long will it take you to scan those farms? 90 hours? But in the case of binary search, after the first farm you will have ruled out 50 farms on the list—one way or another. After the second farm, you will have ruled out another 25. Each time, you are cutting the problem in half. In fact, you can find the dragon after checking only seven farms."

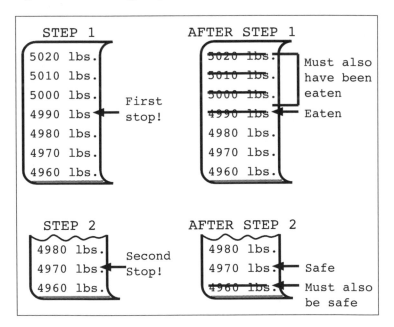

The knight nodded, yet looked unconvinced. "But sir, are you sure?"

The king screamed. "Of course I am sure! I am the king! And, furthermore, every idiot knows that binary search is a logarithmic time algorithm while scanning down a list is a linear time algorithm. *Now go and get that dragon!*"

For the first time in his long career as a knight, Sir Braver ran away. He told himself that he was running in order to carry out the king's orders as quickly as possible. But in truth, the king looked really mad.

As he watched his top knight clank noisily down the hall, the king decided that it was indeed time to go back to bed.

Why Tailors Use Insertion Sort

Insertion sort is a simple, although potentially inefficient, algorithm for sorting an array of numbers. The algorithm iteratively sorts the beginning of the array, expanding the sorted range until the entire array is sorted.

At the start of the ith iteration of the algorithm, the first i numbers in the array are in sorted order. The algorithm then takes the $i + 1$th number in the array, finds the correct location to insert it in the sorted prefix, and inserts it (shifting the following numbers down). Thus, after this step, the first $i + 1$ numbers in the array are sorted.

⌘

"INSERTION SORT!" SCOFFED PETER. Only three months into his apprenticeship at the Library of Alexandria, Peter was already arrogant from the computational knowledge that he now wielded.

"Who would ever use insertion sort?" Peter continued, working himself into a full rant. "It's a quadratic algorithm—$O(N^2)$! You need to learn the wonders of merge sort. I have the scroll right here."

"Oh," remarked the shocked patron, hesitantly taking the scroll. "Thank you?"

"What's going on?" asked the head librarian as he returned from the stacks.

"Your young apprentice was 'educating' me on the correct sorting algorithm to use in my shop," explained the patron.

"He's using insertion sort," added Peter mockingly.

The librarian gave the patron a questioning look, but he didn't burst into laughter as Peter expected.

"I thought you came for a scroll about removing blackberry stains. It took me a while to find that one," said the librarian. Blackberries were out of season and the librarian had had to go deep into the stacks to find the relevant scroll.

The patron nodded. "While I was waiting, I explained to young Peter here how my tailoring shop works. He had some interesting questions about how I sort the jackets."

"Ah," said the librarian. He knew the tailor well. "I think insertion sort makes sense in your case."

Peter was shocked. "What?" he screamed. He felt the blood rise to his face. How could anyone disagree with such a clear difference in computational complexity? That was almost as bad as cheering against the East Alexandria soccer team.

The librarian looked sternly at Peter. Embarrassed, Peter looked down at the floor.

"I don't understand," Peter added quietly.

"Perhaps you should explain how your shop actually works," suggested the librarian.

"It's simple," explained the tailor. "The shop is small, so I only have a single rack for all my jackets. I like to keep them sorted by size, because it's easier when patrons come in. I use binary search to quickly find a jacket in any size I need."

"That makes sense," agreed Peter. Binary search was another one of Peter's favorite algorithms for solving problems. At least the tailor used a reasonable search algorithm.

"Each Monday, I get a new shipment of jackets, which I need to add to the rack. I start by putting them on the end of the rack so they won't sit on the floor and get wrinkled. The new fabrics are finicky this year. I wish wool could have stayed in style a little longer.

"Anyway, after I put them on the rack, I have N sorted jackets at one end and then M new, unsorted jackets after them. So I take each of the new jackets and insert it into the already sorted set of jackets. After inserting the first jacket, I have $N + 1$ sorted jackets and $M - 1$ unsorted jackets. I keep doing this until everything is inserted."

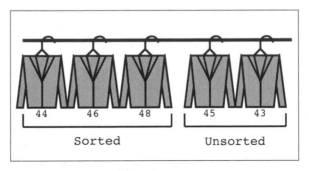

Before Insertion

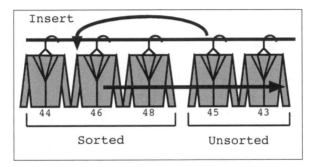

During Insertion

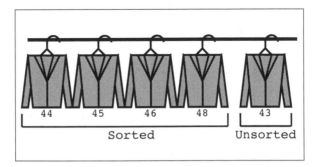

After Insertion

"But—" started Peter. The librarian cut him off.

"I think what Peter wants to know is why you don't take all the jackets off the rack and use something like merge sort," said the librarian. "Other sorting algorithms can be faster."

"Because jackets are heavy," explained the tailor. "It's a pain to take them off the rack. It would be tiring. But the jackets do slide easily down the rack."

Peter looked confused. Why did it matter how hard it was to take things off the rack? This was an argument about computational complexity.

"I think the factor that you're missing is: when most people use insertion sort, the insertions are expensive," the librarian explained to Peter. "Consider an accountant who's trying to sort a list of accounts in one of his books. Each line is one account—like entries in a computer's array. You can't just insert something and have the rest shift down automatically. That would take a most tedious form of magic. Every time the accountant wants to do an insertion, he has to manually shift down everything below that. A single insertion is an expensive $O(N)$ operation. That's a lot of erasing and rewriting.

"But, for a tailor, the insertion is a simple $O(1)$ operation. He pushes the coats down," added the librarian.

Peter nodded an acknowledgement. Inside he chafed at the technicalities of the physical world impacting the cost of different operations. The theoretical world was so much cleaner. However, he did agree with the librarian and the tailor; in this case, insertion sort seemed reasonable. He wondered what other real-world applications might challenge his computational assumptions.

Later that day, Peter tried using insertion sort on several carts' worth of books. Unfortunately, the books didn't move easily between the carts' shelves, and Peter found himself spending the entire night shifting books between shelves. It took him an extra three hours to finish the sorting. He left the library at 2 a.m., angry at himself for not determining the cost of the insertion operation before he started sorting.

Bullies and Bubble Sort

Bubble sort is another simple sorting algorithm. The algorithm repeatedly passes through an array, swapping adjacent elements if they are out of order. As a result, larger elements "bubble" up to the end of the array, while smaller numbers "sink" down. This process continues until the array is sorted. Like insertion sort, bubble sort's worst-case performance is $O(N^2)$.

❧⚬⚬⚬❧

P ETER HAD BEEN IN line for two hours when he felt the tap on his shoulder. He felt a pang of fear as he looked behind him. Terrible Todd glared angrily back. Then again, Terrible Todd always looked angry to Peter.

Terrible Todd was best known for his recent performance at the annual Alexandria-area rock-throwing contest. He had been the first candlemaker's apprentice ever to win the main event. His winning throw had used a two-hundred-pound rock, and the reverberation could be felt two miles away.

Unofficially, he was also known for being a bully.

"Hi Todd," Peter greeted him. His voice came out small, betraying his fear.

Todd grunted back and motioned Peter out of the way. With a strange burst of courage, Peter held firm. He refused to give up his place in line. Season ticket sales for the East Alexandria soccer team started in an hour. This year Peter was determined to get premium season tickets. He had his heart set on midfield.

"I'm sorry, Todd. I was here first," Peter explained.

Todd looked Peter up and down. Then, with a louder grunt, Todd picked Peter up, turned, and set him down behind himself.

"Hey!" Peter cried, but Todd was already tapping the shoulder of the next person in line. Peter briefly considered tapping Todd on the shoulder and confronting him, but he quickly discarded that idea. Peter had seen Todd's winning throw.

Peter fumed. This wasn't fair. Why should Todd get to go in front? There were principles to these things.

As Peter ranted silently in his own head, he watched Todd slowly work his way up the line. One person at a time, Todd swapped places with smaller people. Todd's advance halted only when he reached Wren, the muscular blacksmith.

Then Peter felt another tap on his shoulder. Turning, he saw Big Jim. With a sigh, Peter stepped to the side and let Jim go ahead of him. Like Todd, Big Jim worked his way forward through the line. To Peter's pleasure, Jim even moved in front of Todd to take the spot behind Wren.

Now Tiny Mike stood behind Peter. Peter tried to glare at Tiny Mike, making it clear that Mike wasn't moving ahead. Mike didn't even try.

This process continued for the next hour. Every time a larger person found himself waiting behind a smaller person, there was a tap on the shoulder and a switching of positions. Each time Peter moved back in the line, he felt a little more demoralized. Due to his small size, Peter found himself unable to swap with anyone. By the end of the hour the entire line was sorted by size, with Peter near the back. Discouraged, Peter left the line and returned to the library.

As Peter sulked behind the library's counter, he remembered that this year tickets were also available by pigeon message. He hurriedly filled out the form, requesting "Best Available." He borrowed one of the library's pigeons for the job. The pigeon flapped away, carrying Peter's only hope for reasonable seats.

Ten minutes later, the pigeon returned with a confirmation of second-row, midfield seats. Peter was thrilled. The seat was close to the action and in his favorite peanut vendor's section. He must have purchased his tickets before even Big Jim.

That day Peter learned two important lessons. First, bubble sort is great for bullies. Second, standing in line isn't worth it in the age of near-instantaneous pigeon-based ordering.

Merge Sort and Lines of Kindergarteners

Merge sort is a recursive sorting algorithm based on two intuitive principles:

1) It is easy to sort very short lists. In fact, it is trivial to sort lists containing only one item.
2) It is easier to merge together two sorted lists than to sort a long list.

Using those ideas, the merge sort algorithm can be described simply as: "Break the data in half, sort each half separately using merge sort, and merge the halves back together into a single sorted list." The algorithm is efficient, requiring $O(N \log N)$ time.

A S ANN CONTINUED ALONG the coast toward the city of New Atlantis, she saw a long convoy of ships departing the harbor. She could see the pointers carefully coordinating the convoy's formation with their bright flags, and she again thought back to her first exposure to linked lists in kindergarten. From there, her mind flashed back to other kindergarten memories. She remembered her first game of hopscotch, the annual kindergarten mathematics exam, and the small crabapple tree in the playground. Then, of course, her mind drifted to her teacher.

Ann's kindergarten teacher, Mrs. Magee, was fiercely competitive. She insisted that the class excel in everything. Her class always had the highest test scores. Her class always won at dodgeball. And, most important of all, her class could form a sorted line faster than any other class in the kingdom.

It didn't matter how the class was to be sorted. Mrs. Magee would call out an attribute, and the class would spring into action. The kids could line up by height, by first name, by last name, by length of their left pinky toe, or even by their skill at dodgeball. Truthfully, though, Mrs. Magee avoided sorting by skill in dodgeball, since it often led to heated disagreements and, on at least three occasions, resulted in impromptu one-on-one dodgeball matches.

Like all winning teams, her class's excellence depended on more than natural talent. In fact, most kindergarteners in the class were absolutely dreadful at sorting when they started school. Once, two students, Jack and Jake, had spent fifteen minutes trying to decide which of their names came first in alphabetical order. It was embarrassing.

The class's ability came from practice. Mrs. Magee drilled the class for hours at the start of the school year. Every time the students went to the bathroom or to lunch, she would first make them line up in some sorted order.

Of course, Mrs. Magee also had a strategy—merge sort. It was her secret weapon, her key to winning.

At the command "*Line up!*" the class would split into two groups that were as close to equally sized as possible.

Class before sorting

First split

Those groups would then each split into two smaller groups.

The splitting continued (recursively) until each group contained only a single person.

Then, groups would merge back together in the order in which they split. The merging started with each pair of students, who would merge back into their previous group of two. Each child would look at his or her partner and quickly line up in order. With only two people it was easy. A single quick comparison provided the order.

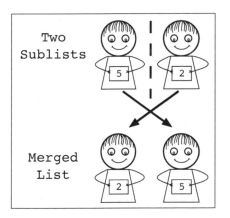

After the groups of two were in order, the kids would merge into larger groups. Again, merging was simple—you only needed to compare the two kids at the front of the two lines. The child with the smallest value had to be one of the first two kids, because the lines were sorted. Or, as Mrs. Magee would say, "If you aren't at the front of the line then you can't come next. So stand still and wait your turn!"

The first two kids would compare, and one would step forward to start the new sorted line.

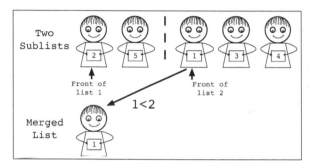

Merge Step I

Then the second smallest still had to be one of the front two kids. And so forth.

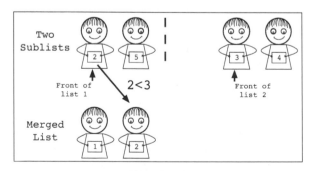

Merge Step 2

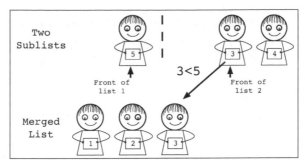

Merge Step 3

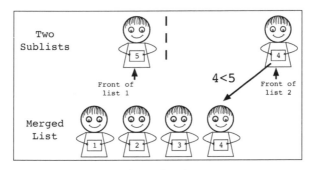

Merge Step 4

Merge Step 5

The lines would quickly merge together, forming larger groups. Each merging step would effectively undo an earlier round of splitting, reforming the group in sorted order. This would continue until the entire class was in order.

That's how Mrs. Magee's class won the sixth annual king-domwide sorting championship. Her class was in order a full five minutes before the runners-up. In fact, Mr. Frizzle's fifth graders were still comparing the numbers of freckles on their right arms when Mrs. Magee's champions left for lunch.

Sorting During the Flu Outbreak

When selecting an algorithm, it is important to understand the context in which it will be applied. An algorithm's computational complexity only tells part of the story. Other factors to consider include the size of the data, the existence of other constraints, and additional problem structure that can be used. For example, bubble sort is a reasonable algorithm to use for a tiny amount of data that is already almost in the correct order.

❧

F OR YEARS, MRS. MAGEE'S KINDERGARTEN class won every sorting competition in the kingdom. The powerful combination of constant practice and the merge sort algorithm made them unstoppable. The class decimated records weekly. Soon Mrs. Magee demanded more than just victory; her class had to finish sorting themselves in less than half the time of their competition. The only true victory was total domination.

Soon Mrs. Magee became overconfident in the ability of her class. She firmly believed that her students could win regardless of the situation, and she had no problem explaining that to everyone she met.

Then, in January, the flu hit. Almost all of Mrs. Magee's class was out sick, leaving just three students. It was under these conditions that Mr. Wallace challenged her to a sorting competition. He also had three healthy students, so the classes were equally matched. But his second-grade class only understood the lesser bubble sort technique. His search could take $O(N^2)$ time!

Mrs. Magee even agreed to allow the children to sort by something simple. After only a moment's thought, Mr. Wallace suggested shoe size.

As soon as the moderator shouted "Go," Mrs. Magee's class split into two groups. One group had two students, and the other had only one student. The merge sort had begun.

In contrast, Mr. Wallace's students looked at each other. Billy and Sue did a quick comparison in their heads and swapped places. All three were now in the correct order.

"No!" wailed Mrs. Magee as she realized what had happened.

It was too late. The competition was over.

The Oracle's Array

Algorithms and data structures are used together to create complex programs. For example, one step of an algorithm might sort the contents of an array, or an algorithm might search for values in a binary search tree.

❧

"THE ORACLE WILL HAVE information," Ann assured herself as she climbed the narrow mountain path. The oracle lived atop one of New Atlantis's taller mountains. Ann had been climbing for eight hours.

Ann chastised herself for not consulting the oracle earlier. While she could blame the long ocean voyage or the treacherous mountain paths, Ann knew the truth. She was afraid to face the oracle. According to legend, the oracle was alternately crazy and mean. Even after arriving in New Atlantis, Ann had spoken to almost a hundred people before seeking the oracle.

As Ann rounded the final corner, she saw the oracle waiting in a chair by the path. The old woman watched her coldly. Ann tried to hide her fear.

After a moment Ann recovered. "Madam Oracle, I've come to ask you for information."

"You want to know about the coming darkness?" asked the oracle. Her voice was raspy and her tone condescending.

"You've seen it?" Ann asked.

"No," answered the oracle. "The quest is obvious. Your father has already consulted every seer in the entire kingdom about it. Except me, of course. He never asked me."

The oracle stared at Ann. Her expression was a mixture of anger, disgust, and the awkward look that some people get right before they burp.

"Why should I help you now?" the oracle asked.

Ann took a deep breadth and started her argument. "The darkness will threaten all of the kingdoms. The fate of the world depends on—"

"Oh, you practiced a speech," cackled the oracle. "I love it when they practice. Did you learn a dance too?"

Ann was taken aback. "Excuse me?"

"Ha!" spat the oracle. "Do you think this is the first time I've heard the 'please save the world' speech?"

"Madam Oracle—" Ann began, but the oracle cut her off with horrible snorting laughter.

After a minute, the oracle calmed down. "What do you want to know?" asked the oracle The laughter had vanished, and she returned to staring at Ann in disgust.

"You'll…help me?" asked Ann, now thoroughly confused by the entire interaction.

"Have you listened to a word I said?" asked the oracle. "I've heard that speech a thousand times. That means I also know you won't leave without getting your precious information. And I want you to leave. Soon."

"Oh," said Ann.

"What do you want to know?" the oracle asked again.

"I want to know about the darkness," said Ann.

"I'm not stupid. We covered that part," responded the oracle. "What do you want to know about the darkness? What it is? How to stop it? Whether it has a favorite poet? I'll only answer one question for you."

Ann responded instantly. "I want to know how I can stop the darkness."

The oracle looked disappointed, but nodded. She shifted

herself from the chair onto the ground and began working. First, she produced a large stack of cards and shuffled them. Then she started laying the cards out on the ground, eight cards in a line. On each card was printed a word in a language that Ann didn't know, an arrangement of bright circles, and a number at the bottom. One of the cards was blank except for the number 999.

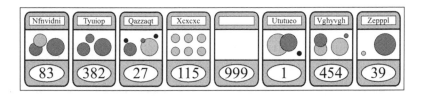

The rhythm of the oracle's motions mesmerized Ann. "While there aren't eight cards on the ground, add another card to the line," Ann muttered under her breath, describing the oracle's motions as a loop. She had no idea why she had said that. Her head suddenly felt cloudy.

The oracle appeared not to notice the statement.

As Ann stared at the row of cards, her perception shifted. She no longer saw a line of eight cards; she saw an array with eight values. The image of a loop iterating over bins in an array filled her mind. Ann shook her head to clear it, but the image remained.

The oracle continued to work. She carefully scooped up all eight cards and began sorting them.

Ann tried to follow what the oracle was doing, but the computational images continued to intrude in her mind.

"What are you doing? You just put those down," asked Ann.

The oracle looked up. "And now I'm sorting them," she stated. "Each card has a number at the bottom. I'm putting them in order." Her tone indicated that she didn't want further interruptions.

Ann watched the sorting with interest. The oracle used a classic merge sort, recursively dividing the pile of cards and then merging them back together. The motions were calm and practiced—almost soothing.

The eight cards, now in sorted order, again formed an array on the ground. The oracle looked at each card in turn while she muttered to herself.

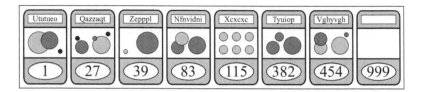

Again, computational imagery flooded Ann's mind. The oracle ceased to be a nasty old woman; instead she became a computer. The cards became an array on the ground. The sorting, pointing, and muttering were parts of an algorithm that Ann didn't understand.

For a brief moment everything seemed to fit in perfect harmony: algorithms, loops, and data structures. Even if she didn't understand the algorithm, Ann was witnessing computation in action. She smiled.

"You will succeed most of the time," said the oracle, her raspy voice snapping Ann out of her stupor.

"Excuse me?" asked Ann.

"The answer," replied the oracle. "You will succeed most of the time."

"What does that mean?" asked Ann.

The oracle shrugged. "How am I supposed to know? I read the answers. I don't always understand them. You asked me how you can stop the darkness and I tell you 'You will succeed most of the time.' That's literally what these words say." The oracle indicated the words printed on the card.

"So you just picked eight random cards, sorted them, and read them off?" asked Ann.

The oracle stared back without answering.

"Well, that answer doesn't help," objected Ann. "How is that supposed to help?"

"You asked the question, and I answered it. Now go away."

Despite a few attempts to argue, Ann was unable to get any more information. Eventually, the oracle grew tired of arguing and hobbled back to her house.

Ann stood on top of the mountain, wondering what the message meant and, more importantly, what to do next.

Big-O and Hitting Things with Hammers

Big-O notation focuses on the (worst-case) performance of the algorithm as the size of the input grows. As such, it focuses on just the aspects of the running time that depend most on the size of the data. Constants are dropped from the Big-O notation.

❧

"**I**'VE DONE IT!" PROCLAIMED Judd as he burst into the library. "I've done it!"

Peter looked up from behind the counter. "Done what?" he asked. He tried to rub the sleep from his eyes.

"I've revolutionized the art of making horseshoes," stated Judd proudly.

Judd was a blacksmith's apprentice in Alexandria and a friend of Peter's. Like all apprentices, he dreamed of making a major contribution to his field—advancing the state of the art. However, as Peter had found, revolutionizing one's field was actually an exceedingly difficult task. His own attempts to improve library science had ended poorly and, in one particularly embarrassing case, resulted in a two-day hospital stay.

"How?" asked Peter.

"It's very technical. What do you know about making horseshoes?" asked Judd.

"Nothing," admitted Peter. He was a librarian's apprentice and had never even been to a forge. When he thought about it, he remembered having once used a hammer. He had been trying to either hang a picture or swat a fly. It was a long time ago, and details were fuzzy now.

"The key is flattening the horseshoe. You have to hit it repeatedly with a hammer until it's flat enough. It takes a lot of muscle."

Peter nodded politely. The description perfectly matched his mental image of blacksmiths pounding metal with large hammers.

Encouraged, Judd continued, "The larger the horseshoe, the more you have to hit it. You need ten hits per inch on each pass. *Ten hits*! But the horseshoe also bulges around where you hit it. So you need to make more flattening passes on longer horseshoes. In fact, for each inch of horseshoe you need to make another pass over the whole thing. So if the horseshoe is N inches long, you need to swing the hammer $10 \cdot N \cdot N$ times."

Judd paused, waiting for some reaction from Peter. After a moment, he added, "For a four-inch horseshoe, that's 160 hits!"

"Wow," responded Peter. It seemed like the correct reaction, but Peter had no idea if that was a lot. After all, blacksmiths hit things all day long.

"You know what I did?" prompted Judd.

"What?" responded Peter with fake interest.

"I found a way to do it in eight hits per inch," Judd stated with a wide grin.

"That's it?" asked Peter. He didn't mean to be rude, but saving two hits per inch didn't seem like a big deal. It was only a constant factor.

"That's a lot," responded Judd. He was obviously upset with Peter for not sharing his joyous moment.

"It's still an $O(N \cdot N)$ process," argued Peter. "Or more accurately it's an $O(N \cdot N \cdot K)$ process to make K horseshoes. I'm guessing that you make more than one horseshoe at a time, right?"

"Huh?"

It appeared that blacksmiths weren't required to learn complexity theory. Peter switched tactics.

"Why not form them in a mold?" asked Peter. "Then it would take $O(K)$ time to make all of your horseshoes."

Judd looked aghast. "It takes hours to make a mold," he protested.

"So?" prompted Peter. "If you make enough horseshoes, it pays off in the long run. That's the beauty of asymptotic complexity: if the problems get large enough the constant factors don't matter and the process with the better asymptotic complexity wins."

Judd didn't look convinced.

"How long does it take to hit the horseshoe?" asked Peter.

"Normally? Or when I'm in the zone?" asked Judd.

"When you're in the zone," answered Peter.

"Two seconds."

"And how long does it take you to build a mold? And cast a horseshoe in that mold?"

"Maybe 15 minutes per inch to carve out the mold, and then 60 seconds to fill the whole mold," answered Judd.

"So to make K horseshoes of size N inches, it would take $2 \cdot 8 \cdot N \cdot N \cdot K$ seconds with your new method. With a mold it would take $60 \cdot K + 900 \cdot N$ seconds. Correct?"

Judd squinted as he tried to confirm the math in his head. His lips moved and he waved his finger as though writing in the air. Peter almost offered him a pen and paper, but worried that this might be insulting.

"So?" Judd asked finally. Peter was not sure if Judd had reached the same conclusion or simply given up.

"In the long run it's cheaper to use a mold," answered Peter. "If you have to make 20 6-inch horseshoes ($K = 20$, $N = 6$), your method takes 11,520 seconds, and the mold takes 6,600 seconds. The mold is faster—a lot faster."

He waited for the look of joy to cross on Judd's face. A simple analysis of computational complexity would save Judd vast amounts of time. But instead of happy, Judd looked angry.

"Fine," he said. "I guess I'll just go make some molds then."

"What's wrong with that?" asked Peter. "Are you upset that I quashed your revolutionary idea?"

Judd shook his head. "No. It's just ... well, I really like hitting things with hammers."

Now Peter could see the problem with the mold idea.

"Oh. Well, no one says that you have to use the most efficient algorithm. Computational complexity just helps you figure out what it is. You can still hit things with hammers, if you prefer."

The smile on Judd's face told Peter that that had been the best news he had received all day.

Graphs

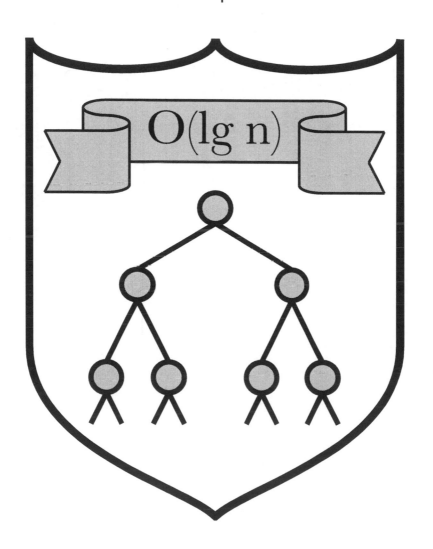

The City of G'Raph

A graph is defined by a set of nodes and a set of edges that link together the nodes. Graphs can be used to represent a large number of real-world systems, including social networks, computer networks, and transportation systems. For example, in a transportation network the nodes could be cities and the edges could be roads between the cities.

❧

A NN ARRIVED AT THE city of G'Raph shortly before nightfall. It looked more like a massive swamp than a proper city. Tiny dirt islands dotted the landscape, poking out of the mud like warts. On each dirt island stood a small structure—usually a house or business. The islands were connected by what appeared to be an inconceivably large number of rope bridges.

Despite the large sign stating "Welcome to G'Raph: Land of the Bridges," Ann was certain that she had arrived at the wrong place. This couldn't be the same G'Raph of which her father had spoken so highly. To hear him tell it, some of the best minds in the world had built G'Raph into an intellectual powerhouse. Could she really find any answers here?

Ann took a deep breath, immediately regretting that decision as the swamp air filled her lungs. She coughed a few times, shook her head in dismay, and walked toward the city. Her first stop was G'Raph's City Hall. She hoped the mayor could introduce her to someone to help with her quest.

Unfortunately, Ann quickly discovered that she couldn't

simply walk to City Hall. Each little dirt island had only a few bridges connecting it to its neighbors, providing her a limited numbers of options of where to go next. This arrangement required her to stop and think about the path, instead of thinking solely about the direction she was going.

Finally, after crossing thirty bridges, Ann stopped at a small farm to ask directions. A small wooden sign on the edge of the property read "Welcome to Thomas's Farm: Home of G'Raph's Best Radishes." The farmer, who had been harvesting his radish crop from the swamp mud, seemed eager to help.

"Excuse me, sir. Can you point me in the direction of City Hall?" asked Ann.

"The direction? I guess it's that way. But you need to take that bridge over there." The farmer's arms extended in different directions.

"Are you sure?" asked Ann. In her experience, the fastest way to City Hall was to walk toward it.

"You're not from around here, are you?" asked the farmer.

Ann shook her head.

"It's the bridges," explained the farmer. "In order to get anywhere in G'Raph, you have to understand how the different islands are connected. Each bridge forms a link between two island nodes. So in order to get from node A to node B, you need to take the correct sequence of bridges."

"I go that way?" Ann asked, pointing away from City Hall.

"You need to go from here to McFane's farm, to the brewery, to the inn, to the 24-hour dry cleaner's, and then to City Hall. That's five bridges." The farmer counted the steps on his fingers.

Ann stared back at him.

"Let me write it down for you," the farmer offered. He pulled out a scrap of paper and sketched a small map:

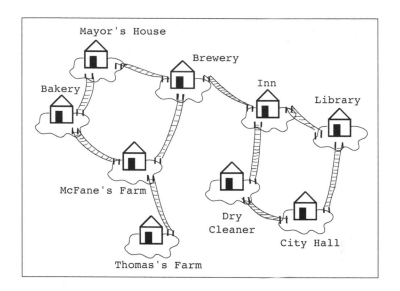

"There you go," he said, offering the paper to Ann. "Each line is a bridge. Just follow the bridges from island to island, and you'll be fine."

"Thank you," Ann said.

Looking at the map, she confirmed that she first needed to walk away from City Hall. Her head spun wildly. How did anyone find their way around here? At least she knew with certainty that Marcus's magic compass would be useless here.

Little did Ann know that the very structure of G'Raph had pushed its population to become a city of algorithmic thinkers. It was here in the city of G'Raph that Ann would find the first real clue to her quest.

Directed Graphs and Bridges

The edges in a graph can be either directed or undirected. Directed edges indicate one-way relationships, such as: there is a link from Node A to Node B. Undirected edges indicate bidirectional relationships, such as that Node A and Node B are linked. The distinction between undirected and directed edges is important to both the structure of the graph and the way algorithms operate on the graph.

A S ANN WAITED IN the mayor's office, she studied the map of G'Raph that hung on the wall. The map itself was huge, taking up the entire south wall of the room. The map contained at least a thousand dirt islands, represented as tiny circles, and several thousand bridges, represented as lines. Each bridge was clearly labeled with some number, which Ann assumed was the distance between islands. At seeing the full extent of the city mapped out, Ann again wondered why anyone would build a city in such an inhospitable swamp.

"Ann!" greeted the mayor in a loud voice. "You've grown so much since I last saw you. It must have been at least ten years. How have you been?"

"I've been splendid. Thank you for asking. And yourself?" responded Ann.

She had absolutely no recollection of ever meeting the mayor. Then again, given how young she was ten years ago, she wouldn't have expected to remember him. Still, Ann was convinced that she should remember this particular man. His bushy gray muttonchops alone would be impossible to forget. They easily covered half of his face.

"I am wonderful," answered the mayor. "Life in G'Raph is most wonderful. How are you finding our humble town so far?"

"I've met the most charming and helpful people. However, I do have to admit that your islands pose a bit of a navigational challenge," answered Ann honestly.

The mayor laughed. He turned to look at the map on the wall. "Yes. That's a common feeling. Luckily, our best scholars have developed some wonderful algorithms. Once a person masters those, life becomes a lot easier."

"I suppose," replied Ann, thoroughly unconvinced.

"You know, it wasn't always this simple, either," continued the mayor in a hushed tone. "My predecessor made such a wonderful mess of our bridge system. He actually made each bridge one-way."

"Really?" Ann gasped. She already knew that it would take a long time to navigate around the city using the bidirectional bridges. The thought of making all the paths one-way was absurd.

"Indeed," answered the mayor. "He thought it would streamline movement. Admittedly, it did make the traffic flow better over each bridge. But it also meant that you had to account for the direction of every bridge when planning your path. Worse though, since each bridge only went one direction, some paths became much too long. He even started building second bridges between some high traffic islands—one bridge from here to there and another from there to here. Perhaps you wondered why there are two parallel bridges between the south market and the top hat shoppe?"

"I didn't come that way, so I didn't have an opportunity to wonder," Ann explained.

"Well, that's why. Before the second bridge, people had to take nine bridges to get to from the south market to the top hat shoppe. It was horrendous!"

"The second bridge helped?" asked Ann.

"It did. However, building extra bridges is too expensive. Unlike adding lines on this map, building a bridge takes real effort. Eventually, we returned to using two-way bridges again."

Ann nodded in agreement. From what she had seen, each bridge probably took days to build. She couldn't imagine it being worth doubling that effort.

Finally, Ann decided to get to the real purpose of her visit. "Sir, my father has always spoken highly of the theorists of G'Raph. I'm sure you're aware of my quest and the vaguely defined danger that the kingdom faces. Would it be possible for me to stay here and learn from your scholars?"

The mayor's face lit up in a wide smile. "Of course!" he proclaimed. "You're welcome to stay as long as you want. I assure you that you shall find our scholars' work most enlightening. I shall take you to the G'Raph library first thing tomorrow."

After thanking the mayor, Ann began her trek back to the inn. As she crossed the bridge from the dry cleaner's to the inn, she was grateful that she could walk either direction across the bridge. She was too tired to find her way around G'Raph through an entirely different set of bridges.

Bridge Weights

Graphs can have either weighted or unweighted edges. In graphs with weighted edges, each edge is associated with a numeric weight. The interpretations of the weights depend on what the graph represents. For example, the weights might indicate the distance between two nodes in a transportation graph, or they could indicate the cost of sending messages between two computers in a computer network.

❧

TWO OF G'RAPH'S SCHOLARS, Edgar and Florence, met Ann at the library. They were both visibly excited. The mayor had warned Ann that G'Raph's academic community rarely had opportunities to show off their latest algorithms, but she had not expected this much energy. The two scholars babbled nonstop about path routing and clustering with such zeal that Ann began to share their excitement.

After settling into a small, overcrowded office in the basement of the library, the scholars immediately pulled out a large stack of maps. Each map showed the same set of islands—the city of G'Raph. However, each map contained different labels next to the bridges.

"What are all these labels?" asked Ann.

"The labels on the nodes or edges?" asked Florence.

"Nodes? Edges?" asked Ann. "I meant the bridges."

"Oh. Sorry," said Florence. "Whenever I look at these maps, I see graph data. Hazard of the job, you know. Each of the islands is a node, and each of the bridges is an edge. So each edge links two nodes. It's a useful abstraction."

"I see," said Ann. "In that case, what do the labels on the edges mean?"

"It depends on the map," answered Florence. "This one is labeled with the distance between the islands. We use it for path planning."

"I understand labeling the bridges with their lengths. That would allow you to compute the shortest path between two islands, right? How else would you label an edge?" asked Ann.

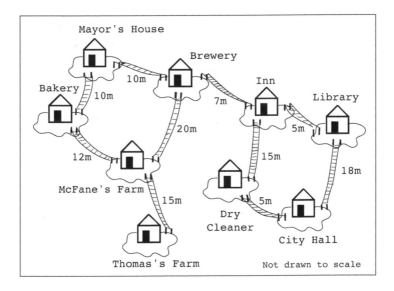

"Distance is only one concern," said Edgar. He had been sitting quietly in the corner, drinking his ninth cup of coffee. "There are hundreds of other things you might want to consider. For example, this map is labeled with the smelliness of each bridge. We use it for planning tours. Some of the bridges cross particularly nasty bits of swamp, you know. We want to avoid those bridges for tours, so we give them a high cost."

"This one is labeled with the estimated length of time needed to cross the bridge," interrupted Florence. She hoped to prevent

Edgar from launching into a coffee-fueled lecture on the unpleasantness of living in a swamp. "We use it to compute different evacuation scenarios."

"Evacuation?" asked Ann in surprise. "Why would you need to evacuate?"

"There was some trouble a few years ago with a dragon," answered Florence. "We didn't account for the time that it actually took to cross an old bridge. It totally gummed up the evacuation. Ten people got stuck at the dry cleaner's after the dragon burned out a bridge. They were trapped for a week."

"And they didn't stop complaining for three months after that," added Edgar.

Ann nodded. The prospect of being stuck at the dry cleaner's for a week seemed rather unpleasant. "Which map do you use most?" she asked.

"This one, of course," answered Florence and Edgar at the same time. They both pointed to a map labeled with the distances between islands.

"You use it for path planning? How do you do that?" prompted Ann. She was eager to learn more about the graph algorithms.

"Dijkstra's algorithm!"

"What's that?" asked Ann. Her knowledge of graph algorithms was admittedly not what it should be.

"You'll love it," said Edgar. "It involves scooters."

Dijkstra's Algorithm on Scooters

Dijkstra's algorithm finds the shortest path from a given starting node to all other nodes in the graph. It requires that the weights of all edges be nonnegative. It operates by maintaining a set of "visited" nodes and continually updating the tentative distance to each unvisited node. At each iteration, the closest unvisited node is added to the visited set and the distances to its unvisited neighbors are updated.

❦

"WE START BY CREATING a list of all islands in the city," began Edgar. "We label them all 'unvisited' and give them a tentative distance of infinity. Except the starting island itself; we give that a distance of zero. You can always get from here to here without moving."

"Distances of infinity are obviously not correct," interrupted Ann. She had walked from the inn to the library this morning, and it hadn't been an infinite distance.

"Of course it's not correct," agreed Florence. "Dijkstra's algorithm keeps finding *shorter* paths to each node. The distance will keep going down as we update our list. Since we haven't found *any* paths at this point, we use the largest distance that we can. That way, any path we find will be better."

That explanation sounded reasonable to Ann. However, she didn't quite see where this was going.

"Then, the fun begins," continued Edgar. "We keep visiting islands until we've visited them all! This is the part where we drive around on scooters."

He took a deep breath before launching into the description. Ann foolishly believed that this was for dramatic effect.

Edgar explained, "At each loop of the algorithm, we follow the same procedure:

1. We find the unvisited island with the shortest distance to our starting point.
2. We travel to that island on our scooters. Usually, Florence and I race. That adds some more excitement.
3. Once we're on the island, we find all of the islands connected to it—all of its neighbors—and update their tentative distances. For each unvisited neighbor, we compute how far it is from the starting island if we go through the current island—that is, the distance to the current island plus the distance to its neighbor. If this new distance is shorter, then we've found a better path and we update the distance.
4. We mark the current island as visited, knowing that we now have the shortest path to that island.

Then we repeat the procedure for the next closest unvisited island."

By the end of the explanation, Edgar was winded. He took a few gulps of coffee as he collected himself.

"At the end, all of the islands have been visited, and we have a list of the shortest distances to each one," added Florence helpfully.

"There's one thing that I don't understand—" Ann started.

"An example will help," interrupted Edgar. "Say we start at the library. That becomes our current node, with distance zero. Everything else starts with an infinite distance."

As Edgar spoke, he retrieved a fresh map of G'Raph from what appeared to be a frighteningly large stack of identical copies of the map. They reminded Ann of children's paper placemats. Edgar circled the library in dark marker.

"Then we look at the neighbors and update their proposed distances," he continued. "In this case, the inn is at most 5 meters away and City Hall is at most 18 meters away."

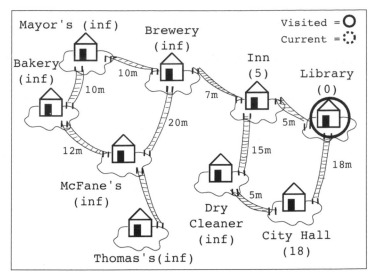

"Now we're done with the library," he continued. "We mark it as 'visited' and move to the next closest island—the inn. In this case, it's a quick scooter drive and not much of a race.

"Since the inn is the closest unvisited island, we know we've found the shortest path to it. We can update both its distance and its path."

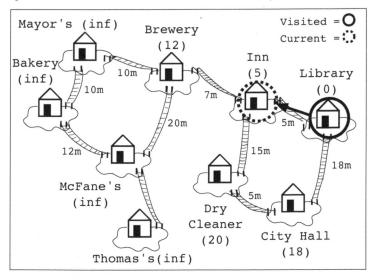

"Yay!" added Florence, cheering on the description of the algorithm.

Edgar gave her a strange look. "Anyway, we do the same thing here: update the neighbors' distances. The inn has three neighboring islands to consider: the library (which is already visited), the dry cleaner's, and the brewery. We update the proposed distance of the dry cleaner's to 20 meters—5 from the library to the inn and 15 from the inn to the dry cleaner's. And we update the proposed distance of the brewery to 12 meters—5 from the library to the inn and 7 from the inn to the brewery.

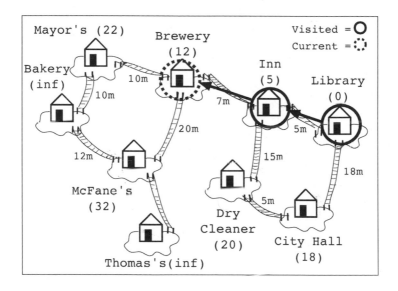

"We again proceed to the closest unvisited node. This time it's the brewery," Edgar explained. "We repeat the process there, updating the neighbors.

"Then, on to City Hall! Here things get interesting. It's a good race from the brewery to City Hall." Edgar made driving motions with his hands as he explained this. "Also, on the algorithmic side, the distance from the library to the dry cleaner's is shorter if we go via the inn instead of via City Hall. So we don't update the distance to the dry cleaner's in this case, because we've already found a shorter path.

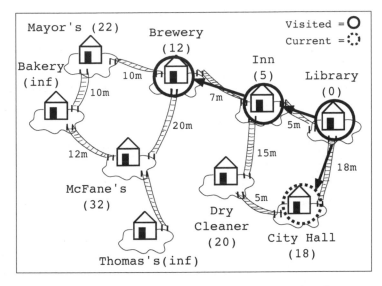

"And so forth," he concluded with a wave of his hand.

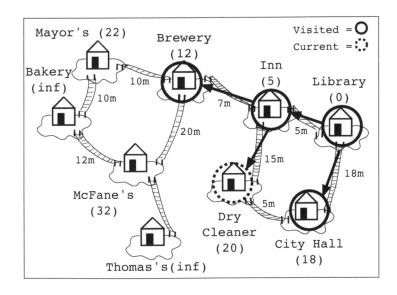

"I understand that part," said Ann. "You expand the set of visited nodes and maintain tentative distances to nodes along the unvisited frontier. Each time you find a shorter path to a node, you use it. What I don't understand is—"

"You're quick!" proclaimed Edgar. "I bet you're confused by the question of whether there could be a shorter path through other unvisited notes?"

"No," declared Ann. "There can't be a shorter path, because you always take the *closest* unvisited node. If there were a shorter path, then it would require going through another node. But we already know that that other node is further away, because it wasn't the closest."

"Why we add the distances, then?" ventured Edgar. "Well, that's simple. The distance of going from A to B through node C is the distance from A to C plus the distance from B to C."

At this point, Ann was severely aggravated at the interruptions. "No! I've walked before. I know that when you walk over two bridges the total distance is the sum of their lengths. And I see that you're ignoring the distance over the island itself, which makes sense given that G'Raph is composed of very little island and a lot of bridge."

Ann continued before she could be interrupted again. "I understand the algorithm. It's all very clear. What I want to know is: why do you have to use scooters? You already have all the distances between islands written on this map. You could do all of this without traveling to the islands."

Edgar looked at Ann blankly. "Why would we do that?"

Ann sighed. "Because it's a lot faster to just mark nodes on a map as 'visited' instead of actually visiting them. You could do this entire algorithm on paper without leaving the library."

Edgar looked at Florence for help. "But scooters are the best part. What fun would it be without scooters?"

Florence agreed. "That's why we call them 'visited' nodes; we get to visit them."

"All I'm saying is that you don't need to actually drive there,"

Ann noted.

"Maybe you're confused about one of the concepts," ventured Edgar. "Let me start again. Dijkstra's algorithm finds the shortest distance from any starting node to all other nodes in the graph. ..."

Ann sighed and sat quietly in the corner. As Edgar and Florence re-explained how to add unvisited neighbors to the visited list, Ann daydreamed about racing through G'Raph on a scooter. There *was* something appealing about that approach.

A Disagreement over Data Structures

Graphs can be represented by a variety of data structures. Two common representations are adjacency matrices and adjacency lists. Both data structures can handle directed, undirected, weighted, or unweighted edges. An adjacency matrix represents a graph as a matrix, with one row and one column for each node. The matrix value of row i, column j is the weight of the edge from node i to node j (0 or 1 for unweighted graphs). An adjacency list maintains a separate list of neighbors for each node.

ANN HAD OBVIOUSLY TOUCHED upon a controversial question. Florence and Edgar stood on opposite sides of the room glaring at each other. The question had seemed innocent enough: "Do you always represent graphs with these illustrations?" Ann had asked.

Florence had quickly answered, "No. Those are only for illustration. Adjacency matrices work better."

Edgar had snapped back, "The correct answer is: adjacency lists."

Silence and glaring had followed.

"What are adjacency matrices and adjacency lists?" asked Ann, starting with the most basic question. Both scholars immediately rushed to explain their data structures. The resulting sound reminded Ann of two chipmunks fighting.

"One at a time, please," Ann pleaded. "Florence, why don't you start with adjacency matrices?"

Florence smiled. "They're simple. Every row represents a node and every column represents a node. If there's an edge between two nodes, you put the edge's weight in the corresponding element. So $M[i][j]$ would store the weight of the edge from node i to node j. Here's an example of some of the islands of G'Raph:

	Bakery	Brewery	City Hall	DryCleaner	Inn	Library	Mayor	McFane	Thomas
Bakery	0	0	0	0	0	0	1	1	0
Brewery	0	0	0	0	1	0	1	1	0
City Hall	0	0	0	1	0	1	0	0	0
Dry Cleaner	0	0	1	0	1	0	0	0	0
Inn	0	1	0	1	0	1	0	0	0
Library	0	0	1	0	1	0	0	0	0
Mayor	1	1	0	0	0	0	0	0	0
McFane	1	1	0	0	0	0	0	0	1
Thomas	0	0	0	0	0	0	0	1	0

"As I mentioned earlier, each island is a node in our graph and each bridge is an edge. In this case, I'm showing an unweighted graph. So a value of 1 indicates that a bridge exists between two islands, and a value of 0 indicates that it does not.

"Adjacency matrices are wonderful. See how it puts all of the information into a single, convenient form? You can even perform some computations by multiplying the matrices."

Ann nodded. It seemed sensible enough.

"Why aren't there ones along the diagonal? Obviously you can get from the library to the library." asked Ann.

"Depending on what you're trying to represent, self edges (or loops) can certainly make sense. In this case, I'm only representing the existence of bridges. There's no bridge from the library to the library," explained Florence.

"Okay. Now Edgar, can you tell me about adjacency lists?" asked Ann, turning to the other scholar.

"Certainly," started Edgar. "You start with a list of the nodes. Imagine a giant array or linked list with the name of each node in it. Then, for each of those nodes, you keep another list of all the nodes to which it connects. For graphs with only a few edges, it can use much less memory. You only store the edges that are there. Here's an example."

Edgar sketched an example on the board that used an array to store the nodes (islands) and a linked list for its neighbors. Ann noticed immediately that, in this case, the existence of an edge (bridge) was implied by the fact two nodes were neighbors. However, the actual ordering of the neighbors didn't seem to matter at all.

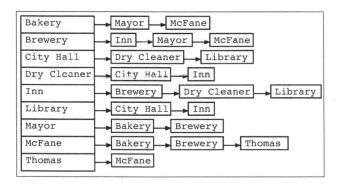

Ann studied the examples. "Both forms can represent the same graph exactly?" asked Ann.

Both scholars nodded.

"Both forms can do directed graphs as well?" asked Ann.

Both scholars nodded.

"They can both represent weighted edges?" asked Ann.

Both scholars nodded.

"Why are you fighting then? It seems like they both do the

same thing, but have different advantages. A matrix is simpler to specify, and a list can take less space. Is that really worth fighting over?" asked Ann.

Both scholars nodded.

"Really?" asked Ann.

"Space matters!" cried Edgar. Then turning to Florence, he asked, "Have you ever tried using your precious matrices to represent the entire pigeon network? There are thousands and thousands of nodes!"

"Simplicity matters too!" answered Florence "I can traverse my matrices with two fixed-size FOR loops. You need to iterate over lists of different size. I've seen your implementations; they have *pointers!*"

"Better to have pointers than a row with ten thousand useless zeros!" responded Edgar.

The argument continued to build. Ann backed away from the two scholars. She was afraid that one of them would throw a coffee mug.

Then, Ann heard a low sigh from the corner of the room. Turning away from the argument, Ann peeked around a huge stack of books. There, at a tiny desk in the corner, sat the most depressed-looking person that she had ever seen. He hunched over his desk, staring at a single sheet of paper on his desk and shaking his head.

"Hello?" Ann said.

The man looked up at her. "Both data structures are completely reasonable in their own way," he explained without bothering to introduce himself.

"I can see that," Ann agreed. "I think they both have advantages and disadvantages."

The man nodded. "I wish they would see that. They make such a terrible racket when they argue. I have important work to do, you know."

"Can I ask what you're working on?"

"It isn't done," he answered. "I haven't figured it out yet."

"What's the problem, then?" Ann probed.

The man didn't answer for a while. Behind her, Ann could hear more shouting. She tried to ignore the argument.

Finally, the man gave Ann a sad look. "It's a really simple problem. I don't know why I haven't been able to come up with a good solution. It really is quite simple. I just want an algorithm that will give me the shortest path through a graph such that the path visits each node exactly once."

"Sounds like a good problem," she offered.

The man nodded. "I've been working at it for a while without any success. It all started a long time ago, when a man in a dark cloak first told me about the problem. I think he might have been a traveling salesman. I never did see his face, though. He told me he had a problem that he needed the best scholar in G'Raph to solve. I was young and naive. I told him I would have an efficient algorithm by the end of the week. That was twenty-five years ago."

The Traveling Salesman's Problem

The traveling salesman problem is a route-planning problem. The goal is to find the shortest path through a graph that visits each node exactly one time and returns to the starting node. The problem is also a classic example of a type of computationally difficult problems called NP-hard. There are no known efficient solutions for solving NP-hard problems exactly, and it has yet to be determined whether or not such solutions even exist.

❦

ANN LOOKED AT THE depressed scholar in the corner. "You've been working on the same problem for twenty-five years?" she asked.

"I'm so close!" he answered.

Behind her, Florence and Edgar had stopped arguing. They peeked their heads around the stack of books.

"Oh. I see you met Geoffrey," said Edgar. "Never mind him."

"I want to hear more about this problem," stated Ann. "What do you mean by 'shortest path'?"

Geoffrey didn't answer. He hunched over his paper and mumbled to himself.

Ann turned back to Edgar and Florence. "You just told me about a shortest-path algorithm," she said.

"This is different," explained Florence. "The traveling salesman problem is a particularly difficult path-planning problem. The goal is to find the shortest path through a graph that visits each node exactly once and returns to the starting node."

"Here are two example paths through G'Raph's school neighborhood," offered Edgar, drawing a crude sketch on a nearby blackboard.

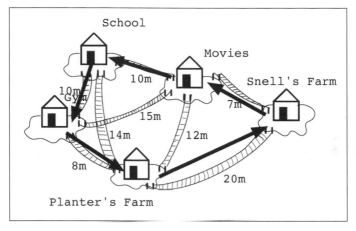

Path 1

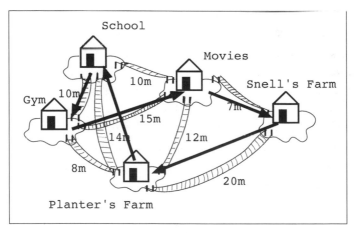

Path 2

"Both paths cross each node exactly once. Path 1 has a distance of 55 meters, and path 2 has a distance of 66 meters," he explained.

"That seems simple enough," commented Ann. "There's really no algorithm to solve it? Why not try all possible orderings of nodes? For each ordering, you could compute the total distance traveled if you visited the nodes in that order."

"There's no known *efficient* algorithm to solve it," explained Edgar. "No exact solution, at least. The method you suggested would work, but it's factorial, $O(N!)$. For the five nodes in our simple example, there are $5! = 120$ different permutations."

Florence shrugged. "No one actually knows if there's an efficient solution or not. At least no one has found an efficient solution yet. There are good approximations, of course, but no exact algorithm."

"I played with it for a while," offered Edgar. "I never made much progress."

"Geoffrey has been working on it for twenty-five years?" asked Ann.

Both scholars nodded. "Ever since he met that man, Geoffrey has been unnaturally obsessed with this problem. He doesn't think about anything else. In the past, he would work on three or four different problems at the same time. It's as though he's under some sort of spell," Edgar explained.

Edgar's words sent a shiver through Ann. A vague memory floated through the back of her mind, but she was unable to latch onto it.

"Has anyone else met that man?" Ann asked.

Edgar shrugged. "I don't think so. Geoffrey said that he was probably a visiting salesman."

"He was selling questions," Geoffrey said quietly. Ann jumped at the sudden statement. Even though she had spoken to him only a minute ago, she had forgotten he was there.

"What did he look like?" asked Ann. The undefined memory continued to nag at the back of her mind.

"Dark cloak and a large wooden staff that was covered with mathematical symbols," answered Geoffrey. "Never did see his face, though."

"You only saw him that one time? Twenty-five years ago?" she confirmed. Why should an event from twenty-five years ago bother her now?

"Three times," answered Geoffrey. "The first time was twenty-five years ago. Then I saw him again ten years later. I was about to give up on the problem, but he found me and asked if I had solved it. That question rekindled the fire. I knew I could find a solution."

"And the third time?" asked Ann. She could feel a pit of fear building inside her, but she wasn't sure why.

"This morning," mumbled Geoffrey. "As I walked by the school, I saw him talking to some girl. He stopped for a moment and waved with his staff. I still haven't found a solution, so I kept walking. I know I can find one. I'm so close."

Ann didn't wait for the rest of the story; she ran out the door and toward the school.

Panicked Depth-First Search

Depth-first search is a search algorithm that fully explores a single path before backtracking to test other paths. The algorithm operates recursively, using a depth-first search to explore all of the options down one subpath before considering other subpaths.

A NN REALIZED HER MISTAKE as soon as she crossed the first bridge. In her rush to get to the school, she had neglected to bring a map with her. In any other town, this wouldn't have been a problem—she would have run in the general direction of the school. But traveling in G'Raph wasn't that simple.

Ann stopped when she reached Thomas's farm. Two paths branched out in front of her without any indication of which one led to the school. She looked for Thomas, but the farmer wasn't in his radish patch.

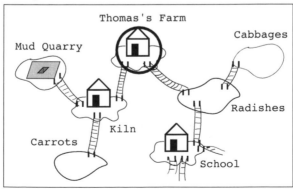

Making a quick decision, Ann chose the path on her right. She ran over the bridge and found herself at a pottery kiln. An assortment of bowls lined shelves outside the kiln. Judging from the quality of craftsmanship, some of the bowls must have been made by third graders at the school. Ann hoped that she was getting close.

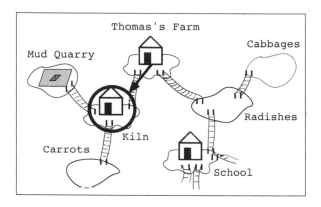

Ann had another decision to make two new paths led away from the kiln. Again, Ann chose the path to her right, and she ran over the bridge. This time, she hit a dead end. The island, which appeared to be a mud quarry, had no new bridges that might lead to the school.

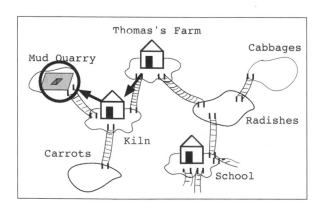

Ann backtracked quickly, returning to the pottery kiln island.

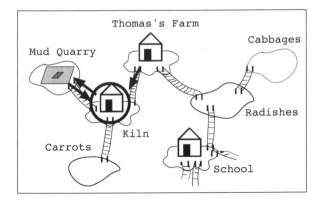

She ran down another bridge, arriving at a carrot farm—another dead end.

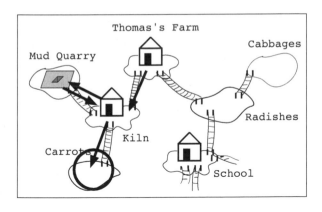

Ann backtracked to the pottery kiln again. This time there were no new paths to take, so she backtracked further. She returned to Thomas's farm.

From the farm, she took the other bridge and arrived at another (smaller) radish farm. From the looks of it, this farm was decidedly less successful than Thomas's farm. Ann paused for the briefest moment to wonder what could cause the difference in radish-growing performance between two almost indistinguishable islands of mud. She quickly pushed that question out of her head and continued her search.

Yet again, Ann faced a choice of bridges. She started with the path to her right. Much to her relief, this bridge led to the school.

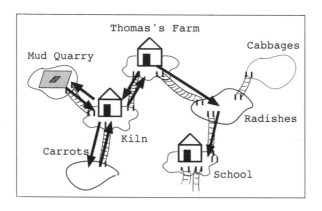

Ann ran up to the school, where Florence and Edgar now waited. Edgar held a folded map of G'Raph in his hand. Ann cursed herself again for not having brought her own map. She could have avoided a lot of backtracking.

"You made it!" exclaimed Edgar. "I was afraid you would get lost without a map."

"I did get lost," admitted Ann. "Or, at least, I hit a few dead ends and had to backtrack."

"Ah, a depth-first search," noted Florence. "Nice."

"Depth-first search?" asked Ann, a little out of breath from all the running.

"Depth-first search is when you keep exploring along one path until you hit either a dead end or a node that you've seen before. Then you backtrack to the most recent decision point and try a different option. If there are no new options at that point, you backtrack again." Edgar explained.

"With depth-first search, you keep exploring deeper and deeper until you come to a dead end," added Florence.

"Or find what you're looking for," added Edgar.

"Good point," replied Florence. "You can also find what you're looking for. Edgar, remember that time we used depth-first search on that choose-your-own-adventure novel?"

"Fun times," answered Edgar. He looked off into the sky as though replaying the memory in his mind.

Ann was too tired to appreciate the algorithmic beauty of her own frantic run. A map would have saved her from experiencing depth-first search firsthand.

The school's principal, having seen the group standing outside, came out to investigate.

"Excuse me," he said in the stern tone every principal seemed to have mastered. "Who are you and why are you here? If you're selling flashcards, you can keep walking. We don't buy from traveling flashcard salesman."

"Have you seen a strange man in a dark cloak?" asked Ann without bothering to introduce herself or answer any of his questions.

"Umm, yes. Why do you ask?" asked the principal.

"Did he talk to anyone?" asked Ann, again ignoring the principal's question.

"He talked with one of our star students, Elizabeth," answered the principal. "He had some question about some sort of math problem. I was there, too, but honestly I couldn't understand what he was talking about.

"Elizabeth seemed certain that she could figure it out, though. She went right home to work on it. She's bright, you know. Probably the best scholar that our school has ever taught. She'll find the answer."

"Do you know what the question was?" asked Ann.

"It was something about islands and bridges. I think he called it 'vertex covering.' I hadn't heard of it before, but it sounded like fun."

"Another classic NP-hard graph problem," said Edgar cheerfully. "I worked on that one too."

Ann felt her stomach drop.

Now Elizabeth, G'Raph High School's star student, had become singularly obsessed with it. She had fallen victim to the same spell as Geoffrey.

The wizard had targeted two star scholars. Unfortunately, Ann had no idea why.

Bridge Upgrades

The minimum spanning tree of an undirected graph is the smallest set of edges such that all of the nodes are connected (if possible). Similarly, in a weighted graph, the minimum-cost spanning tree is the set of edges with the minimum total weight that connect together all the nodes.

A NN WENT STRAIGHT TO City Hall, where she hoped to find more information about the mysterious wizard. Florence and Edgar decided to join her. Or, more accurately, they decided to demonstrate how quickly they could navigate G'Raph on their scooters. At least they left their map with Ann.

Ann found the mayor in his office, staring intently at a map of G'Raph.

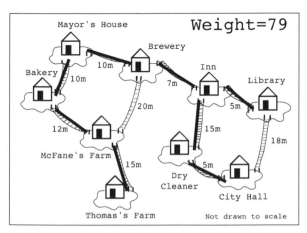

"Mayor, I have an important question for you," started Ann.

The mayor didn't acknowledge her. He continued to stare at the map, mumbling to himself. He appeared to be tracing different paths with his finger. Ann started to panic. Had the wizard been here?

After a moment, the mayor finally turned. "Edgar, this will never do. You need to redo it," he snapped.

"What?" asked Edgar. "That's exactly what you requested: the minimum-cost spanning tree."

"The what?" asked the mayor with a confused look.

"Umm, I have an important question here," tried Ann, but nobody was paying attention.

"It's the set of bridges to upgrade," Florence explained to the mayor.

The mayor stood silently, not making the connection.

Florence continued. "You asked for the cheapest set of bridges to upgrade such that you could travel between any two islands while only crossing stone bridges. Since the price is determined by the length of the bridges, we found the shortest set of bridges."

"Why would you need to connect all the islands with stone bridges?" asked Ann, forgetting her original question for the moment.

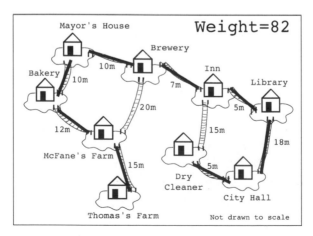

"Nobody wants to be stuck at the dry cleaner's after a dragon attack," said Florence without additional explanation.

"We need a stone bridge between City Hall and the library," said the mayor.

"That would add another three meters," responded Edgar. "It's cheaper to connect the inn and the dry cleaner's." He pointed to the relevant bridges on the map to illustrate.

The mayor started to argue, but Ann cut him off.

"Interesting," interrupted Ann. "You found the set of bridges to replace that will connect all the islands together, while minimizing the total cost. Did it take you long?"

"No," answered Florence. "I used Prim's algorithm."

"Prim's algorithm?" asked Ann.

"It's a relatively simple algorithm," said Florence. "You start with a random node and add it to a new set of connected nodes. In this case, I 'randomly' chose the library."

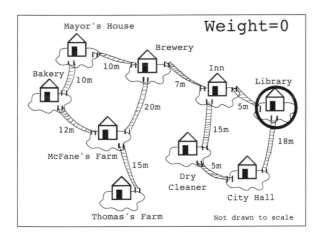

"Then you keep adding the closest node that isn't already in the set. Since we want to minimize the cost of each new edge, we define 'closest' to use the distance from the node to any node in the set. In this case, we first add the inn, which is five meters from the library."

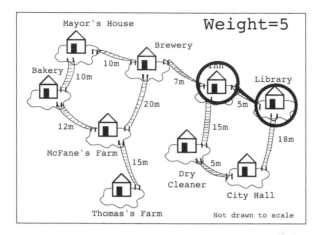

"Then the brewery, which is seven meters from the inn."

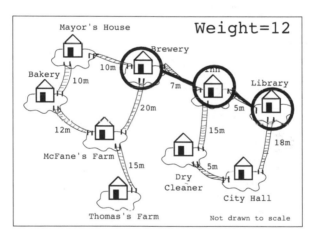

"All very fascinating," interrupted the mayor. "But the library and City Hall should have a new stone bridge between them."

"Edgar and Florence are correct," said Ann. "The minimum-cost spanning tree doesn't have a new bridge there."

"But...I walk that way every day," said the mayor. "I'm tired of the wobbly old bridge. We need something new."

Edgar, Florence, and Ann all looked at each other. Edgar took a deep breath to start another algorithmic argument, but thought better of it. It was obvious that an algorithmic argument wouldn't sway the mayor. Edgar decided to submit both prices and let the mayor choose.

Suddenly remembering why she had gone to the mayor's office in the first place, Ann spun toward the mayor.

"Mister Mayor, I think there's a wizard casting a spell on the scholars of G'Raph," Ann blurted out. "I think the city and all of its scholars are in danger."

Behind Ann, Edgar and Florence gasped in unison.

The Game of Hamiltonian Paths

A Hamiltonian path visits each node in a graph exactly one time. The problem of determining whether a graph has a Hamiltonian path is NP-hard.

❦

"MISTER MAYOR, I THINK there's a wizard casting spells on the scholars of G'Raph," Ann repeated. "Everyone to whom the wizard has spoken has become obsessed with finding an efficient, exact solution to a specific NP-hard problem. Have you heard any stories about a stranger in a dark cloak asking scholars NP-hard computational problems?"

The mayor looked confused. "NP-hard? I'm not exactly sure what that means, but I had a man in a dark cloak ask me a hard question once."

"You did?" asked Ann, Edgar, and Florence in unison. None of them could hide the shocked looks on their faces.

"Yes," answered the mayor. "It was about twenty years ago—right after I left school. He had just come from the library. I think he stopped to talk to Geoffrey about some salesman problem. Geoffrey was my favorite teacher, you know. He would always have the easiest tests. Anyway, the man asked me if I could solve a game: find a path through G'Raph such that I go through each island at most one time."

"The Hamiltonian Path problem," stated Edgar. "It's also NP-hard."

"It's related to Geoffrey's traveling salesman problem," added Florence.

"But why did the wizard ask *you* about Hamiltonian paths?" Ann asked, trying to phrase the question tactfully. From her limited time with the mayor, he had yet to strike her as one of G'Raph's great scholars.

The mayor shrugged. "I don't know, but it sounded like a fun game."

"It's a popular game in G'Raph," Edgar agreed. "We played Hamiltonian paths as kids. We would draw out different hopscotch graphs and have to traverse them in Hamiltonian paths. Of course, you weren't allowed to solve them ahead of time. You had to determine the Hamiltonian path *as you were hopping*. If you got stuck or stepped on the same node twice, you were out."

Ann looked skeptical. "You really played that as a kid? That was how you spent your childhood?" she asked.

Edgar smiled at the fond memory. "Those were good times," he answered.

"What did you say to the wizard?" Ann asked the mayor. "You didn't solve it, did you?"

The mayor smiled. "I sure did. I told the man in the cloak: 'That's easy. I would just build a few more bridges.' The man left shortly after that. I think he said something about my future as a politician."

"That's cheating," objected Edgar. "You can't add bridges in a game of Hamiltonian paths!"

"Mister Mayor," interrupted Ann. "Do you know anyone else who met the wizard?"

The mayor thought for a moment. "Not here in G'Raph. But I had an intern who told me a story that sounded similar to what you're claiming. He had a good friend in the town of Bool who became obsessed with one of these hard problems. What did you call them? NT? ND?"

"NP," offered Ann.

"Sure, sure. Anyway, my intern's friend had a fun little problem called 3-SAT or something like that. Sounded like the type of thing you would find in the Sunday paper."

"The town of Bool? Are you sure?" asked Ann.

The mayor nodded. "You always know a Boolean when you meet one."

Ann couldn't agree more. At the thought of Bool, her mind flashed back to Dr. Conjunctione and his insistence on solving 3-SAT. In that instant, the scope of the problem became frighteningly clear.

After a few more minutes of discussion, Ann decided that she wasn't going to find any more answers here. She knew that there was a wizard who was casting spells on computational scholars; now she had to figure out why.

For the first time in her quest, Ann knew where to go next. She needed to pay a visit to the one place where she might find more information about NP-hard problems: the Library of Alexandria.

Computational Thinking

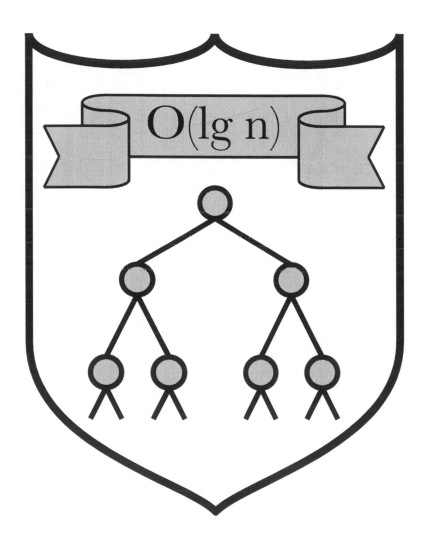

Reflections on Algorithms

Complex algorithms build on a core set of fundamental concepts. Mastering these basic concepts and learning to combine them is the key to solving new problems.

❧

F OR THE MILLIONTH TIME, Ann wished that she had a better algorithm for solving quests. She wanted something that required less guessing and that guaranteed a solution. Most of all, she wanted something fast. After nearly a year of searching, Ann was tired.

As she looked down at the rugged dirt road, her mind wandered back to her time at G'Raph and the algorithms she learned there. Those algorithms, such as Dijkstra's shortest-path algorithm and Prim's algorithm for minimum spanning trees, went beyond anything that Ann could have imagined a year ago. Yet these new algorithms used concepts Ann had learned in first grade.

Dijkstra's shortest-path algorithm was based on a few simple loops:

WHILE there are unvisited nodes ...

FOR each of the neighbors of the current node ...

Similarly, Prim's algorithm was just a loop that added new nodes to a set until there was nothing left to add. It also required updating and finding "close" nodes.

Everything she learned in G'Raph built on the core set of

computer science concepts she had learned in school. As this realization struck Ann, a burst of hope flowed through her. She had the tools to solve this quest. Now she needed to figure out how to apply them.

Computational Graffiti

Recursion can allow a complex algorithm to be specified in a short, simple, and often beautiful form. A function calls itself on a subset of the data, using the results from those subproblems to form the final solution. However, recursion can also add computational overhead due to the new recursive function calls.

❧

WHILE TRAVELING TO THE Library of Alexandria, Ann could see the signs of chaos engulfing the kingdom. The traditionally smooth operation of the kingdom's services barely squeaked along under the burden of additional complexities. Overhead, the pigeons of the kingdom's vast carrier network flew about aimlessly. The postal carriers had stopped sorting the mail before embarking on their delivery routes. Instead, they stood in front of each mailbox and flipped through their full bags to find that house's letters. Everything was a mess.

Ann first noticed the computational graffiti in the outskirts of Alexandria. Initially, it looked harmless—the rebellious proclamations of teenagers: "DFS rulez" or "Dynamic Programming FTW." However, the signs soon became more troubling: "Say 'No' to Big-O" and "BRUTE FORCE ALGORITHMS FOREVER."

At first, Ann thought these signs were jokes. Who would argue against an efficient algorithm? The absurdity made them almost amusing.

Then, Ann saw a message that stopped her cold:

```
int RecursiveAdd(int n, int m) {
   if (m == 0) return n;
   return RecursiveAdd(n, m-1) + 1;
}
```

The recursive algorithm for adding two numbers covered the entire north wall outside a florist's shop. It was written in the classical language of C, which Ann had learned in school. While it was technically valid, the sheer inefficiency of the approach shocked Ann.

For example, given $n = 10$ and $m = 5$, the function would be called a total of six times!

User calls: RecursiveAdd(10, 5)

Recursive call: RecursiveAdd(10, 4)

Recursive call: RecursiveAdd(10, 3)

Recursive call: RecursiveAdd(10, 2)

Recursive call: RecursiveAdd(10, 1)

Recursive call: RecursiveAdd(10, 0)

Mercifully, the recursive chain would stop after the sixth call. The last call would return 10. The next call would add 1 to that result and return 11. This process would continue to work its way back up until the top level function returned $(10 + 4) + 1 = 15$.

Why take a simple mathematical operation, $m + n$, and specify it as a chain of $m + 1$ function calls? The overhead was staggering. The graffiti clearly pointed to the complete collapse of computational thinking.

Tearing herself away from the disturbing image, she broke into a full run. There was no time to lose.

The NP-Hard Curse

NP-hard is a class of computational problems for which there are no known efficient and exact algorithmic solutions.

❧

$\mathbf{B}$ Y THE TIME ANN arrived at the Library of Alexandria, things had deteriorated further. She heard reports from throughout the kingdom of people falling victim to an obsession with specific NP-hard problems. It appeared that over eighty percent of the kingdom's top scholars had been cursed. Most recently, Ann had learned that the Bureau of Farm Animal Accounting: Large Mammal Division—the greatest collection of complexity theorists in the kingdom—had fallen. The nine theorists, including Clare O'Connell, had vanished.

"I need everything that you have on NP-hard problems, computational complexity ... and curses," ordered Ann as she approached the main desk.

Peter, the librarian's apprentice, looked worried. "Everything?"

"Everything," confirmed Ann.

A look of panic replaced the worry on Peter's face. "Are you here to curse me?" he asked. Then, with more resolve, he puffed out his chest and declared, "I will protect the wisdom in the Library of Alexandria with my life!"

Ann froze in surprise. It never occurred to her that she might be mistaken for the very wizard that she needed to stop. However, judging from the young librarian's reaction, he seemed certain that she was here to destroy the scrolls, curse him, or, at the very least, add to the already plentiful graffiti.

"Umm, no. I'm not here to curse you or do anything bad to the library. I'm Princess Ann. I was sent by my father, King Fredrick, to stop the coming darkness. I need your help."

The panic on Peter's face melted into relief. The relief gave way to gleeful excitement, which produced its own scary sort of expression. Peter's entire face was contorted into a massive smile, and he seemed to have stopped blinking. Ann wished he could have stayed at relief.

"I can help!" Peter cried as he turned and ran into the stacks.

He returned fifteen minutes later carrying ten scrolls, two books, and an ancient clay tablet. "Here's the first batch. I brought these up now so you can get started. Unfortunately, this is the type of request where our caching system doesn't work too well."

"Caching system?" asked Ann, but Peter had already disappeared back into the stacks.

Ann took the scrolls over to a table in the corner. As she worked, Peter returned with new batches of scrolls. Ann noticed that over half the scrolls on computational complexity were from the Bureau of Farm Animal Accounting.

All together, about one hundred scrolls covered the table before Peter finally paused for a moment. He breathed heavily from the constant running, and sweat dripped from his nose.

"What are you looking for?" he asked over the mountain of material.

"I'm not sure," Ann answered, wondering why he hadn't asked this question sooner. "Anything that might help me understand this curse or its purpose."

"I heard that the curse targets scholars and forces them to become obsessed with NP-hard problems to the exclusion of all else. One thinker was helping the navy rewrite their manuals to use functions, but he became obsessed with packing cargo into the ships' holds. They say he now lives in the cargo hold of a cow-transport ship in hopes of being inspired," Peter babbled, his energy returning.

Ann winced at the story. It had been her request that had sent that scholar to help the navy. She wondered if he would have otherwise avoided the curse. She tried to push that doubt from her mind and refocused on the problem.

"What's all the excitement over NP-hard problems anyway?" asked Ann.

Peter gasped. "NP-hard problems are some of the hardest problems in the world," he explained. "Everyone wants to solve them! You would be rich and famous!"

"Why?" asked Ann.

"Because no one has figured out an efficient algorithm for them yet," answered Peter. "You can always check whether you have a valid solution, but generating an exact solution from scratch is much harder."

Ann continued to look unimpressed.

"Take the problem of Hamiltonian paths," Peter continued. "You need to find a path through a graph that touches each node one time. It's really easy to check if any given path is valid—you simply test the path. Does it step on the same node twice? Yet it's incredibly hard to even determine whether any such path exists."

"Is it that important?" asked Ann. "I guess the Hamiltonian path problem is interesting, but solving it won't cure the common cold."

"It's very important!" exclaimed Peter. "Well, maybe not Hamiltonian paths themselves, but solving these types of NP-hard problems. They have real, practical applications. Further, some NP-hard problems can be reduced to different NP-hard problems. That means if you solve one problem, you can solve another. If you found an efficient, exact solution to the Hamiltonian paths problem, you would find a solution to the 3-SAT problem. It would revolutionize everything."

"Oh," Ann said. She had never really appreciated the scope of these problems. "And it's hard to solve these problems?" she asked.

"Over three-quarters of the kingdom's best scholars are

spending every waking moment on them now with no luck. So ..."
Peter trailed off.

"We need to figure out how to break the curse," finished Ann.

Everyday Algorithms

Algorithms are essential for thousands of everyday tasks. We use algorithms for everything from adding two numbers together to navigating a store.

❧

PETER WATCHED ANN FOR ten minutes before he had the courage to disturb her. Even then, it took him five false starts to get the words out. If Ann hadn't been so absorbed in her work, she would have found the entire incident creepy.

"Excuse me," Peter ventured.

Ann looked up, dazed. "What?"

Even though her tone was pleasant, the words sent a wave of guilt through Peter. He had been trained not to disturb patrons unless there was a fire or the library was about to close. Stopping Ann's research for a question seemed terribly rude.

"Do you know what 'the darkness' is? Is it the curse?" he asked. "I only ask because it could help me locate other resources for you. The master librarian has said that I should make helping you my top priority."

"I'm not sure, but I think 'the darkness' refers to a new dark age. A computational dark age, to be exact."

"Computational dark age?"

"The wizard appears to be targeting the computational thinkers, and clearly the kingdom is already suffering."

Something didn't sound right to Peter. "Does it matter that

much?" he asked.

"Excuse me?" asked Ann. "Have you seen the graffiti? The cursed scholars? The wandering tribes of bureaucrats?"

"I mean, it seems like a lot of problems to result from a curse on scholars."

"Algorithms," Ann said. Her entire face came to life, and Peter could hear the passion in her voice. "Algorithms are everywhere. The entire kingdom runs on algorithms."

Ann set a scroll down on the table and continued, "Consider something as small as adding two numbers; it's an algorithm. You add the two rightmost digits. Then the next two. Then the next two. It's a loop over the digits—right to left. And there are specific steps for each digit. You add the numbers, determine whether you need to carry one to the next column, and so forth. It's an algorithm."

"I meant new algorithms," Peter managed to interrupt. "The impact of new algorithms."

Ann switched topics seamlessly. "There's always the need for new algorithms. Sometimes you need to solve a new problem, or solve an old problem more efficiently. The scholars I met in G'Raph worked on these types of new algorithms daily. Or sometimes there's a real-world twist to a known problem that requires you to adapt the solution. The importance of continued algorithmic development should not be underestimated."

At the mention of adapting the algorithm for the real world, Peter flashed back to his own experience with insertion sort. He shook that thought out of his head and tried again.

"That isn't what I meant," he said. He waited a moment, not providing Ann a new topic on which to rant.

Ann looked back at him. "Then what did you mean?" she asked.

"The wizard has cursed all of the scholars, so they aren't developing any new algorithms. I get that, and that's bad. But why is it impacting everything else so quickly? It should take a while for the kingdom to get this bad, right? Not everyone needs a new algorithm every day. It's not like a loaf of bread in a damp closest.

Algorithms don't get all green and fuzzy with age."

"Oh, right…that," said Ann, the energy draining out of her voice.

Ann didn't speak for a moment. She looked at Peter, carefully studying him. Peter got the distinct feeling that he wouldn't like what came next.

"It's much worse than that," Ann said finally.

"Worse?" asked Peter.

"Worse," confirmed Ann.

"Uh, how?" asked Peter nervously.

"I think the spells are targeting more than the scholars," explained Ann. "The curse is seeping into all aspects of life. It's using the scholars—using them to target the very algorithms themselves. You curse an expert in sorting, and you curse the sorting algorithm itself. The wizard is unraveling the very basis of computation in the kingdom."

"Oh," was all that Peter could manage. His legs suddenly seemed a bit wobbly. He felt around for a chair, pulled it behind him, and fell into it.

"Oh," he repeated.

"Yeah," Ann agreed.

"So?" asked Peter.

"I have to stop it…fast."

The Quicksort Message

Quicksort is a recursive sorting algorithm that is similar to merge sort. Like merge sort, quicksort partitions the items into two groups, recursively sorts those groups, and merges the results into a single sorted list. Unlike merge sort, quicksort uses the items' values in the partitioning. Quicksort chooses a random element, called a pivot, and divides the current list into two sublists: items less than or equal to the pivot, and items greater than the pivot. Since the lists are partitioned by value, the merge operation consists of simply appending one sorted list to the other.

The worst-case performance of quicksort is $O(N^2)$. However, quicksort takes $N \log N$ time on average. In fact, quicksort can be faster than other $O(N \log N)$ sorting algorithms such as merge sort.

❧

"WHAT ARE YOU DOING?" asked Ann.

"Putting away books," answered Peter. "We ask the patrons to leave the books out for us, because they always mess things up when they try to help. They take the book back to the general area where they got it, see a gap, and shove it there. It messes up the whole order. And you should see what they do with the scrolls."

"Okay," agreed Ann. "But what are you doing with the those books now?"

"Sorting them," answered Peter. "It's easier if I sort them here. That way I can go through the stacks in order and put away the books. It's like the merge step of a gigantic merge sort. It saves a lot of time."

"But *how* are you sorting them? It almost looks like you're picking things at random."

"Oh," Peter said. "This is something new that an accountant showed me. She called it quicksort. It has a terrible worst-case big-O complexity, but it actually works pretty well."

"An accountant?" asked Ann.

"I think she works for a farm animal bureau, but she seemed to understand sorting. She obviously isn't a computational expert though, or she would have known this quicksort has a worst-case time of $O(N^2)$. Imagine trying to sort more than a few shelves of books—"

"Clare O'Connell?" interrupted Ann. She stood up, staring intensely at the book cart.

Peter paused. In the five days Ann had been working at the library, she had barely looked up from her books. Her sudden interest in the reshelving of books unnerved him. The fact that she was paying any attention to *him* now was unnerving.

"That sounds familiar," Peter answered hesitantly.

"Tell me everything," commanded Ann. She stood next to him now, still staring at the bookshelves. "What did she say?"

"Uh, okay...yeah, she was in here a few weeks ago to get a scroll on cows—or turkeys—or some type of animal. I'm pretty sure it was cows, though."

"What about the sorting?" prompted Ann.

"All she said was that there was a better way to sort," Peter said. "She showed me this algorithm that she called quicksort. You start with a stack of books to sort. Pick one book at random. You call that the pivot book.

"Then you use the pivot to split the stack into two smaller stacks. Books before the pivot go on the left and books after the pivot go on the right.

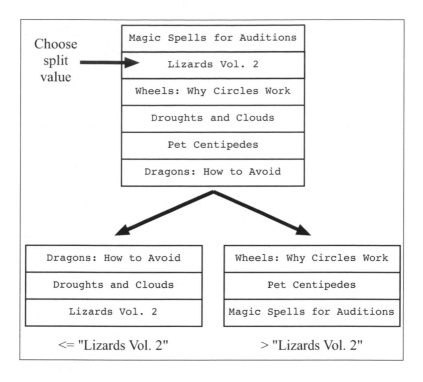

"You keep recursively splitting piles until you have one book in each pile.

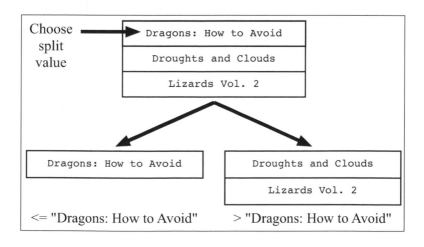

"Then you merge them back together by putting the left pile in front of the right pile."

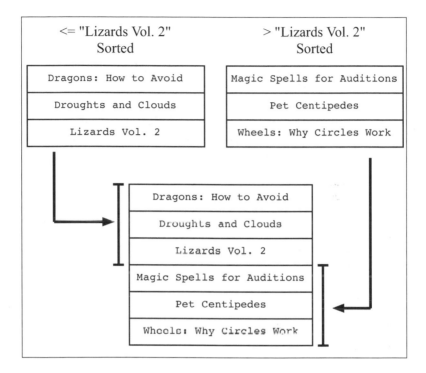

Peter shrugged. "That's all there is. As I said, it's worst case $O(N^2)$, but it usually goes faster than that. More importantly, it's a lot easier to merge library books by putting one pile on top of another."

Ann didn't respond. She continued to stare at the shelf of library books. Finally, she whispered, "It has an $N \log N$ expected running time."

"Expected?" asked Peter.

"It means that *on average* it will take $N \log N$," answered Ann. "I heard rumors that Clare was working with expected running times."

"The worst case is still N^2," objected Peter. He firmly believed that worst-case running time spoke for itself.

That broke Ann out of her trance. "That's the beauty of it," answered Ann. "You would need to always make a bad pick to have a that bad a running time. For example, if you always chose the smallest value for the pivot, it would be bad. You would need to split the books N times, with each split requiring up to N comparisons."

Ann turned back to the bookshelf. Her voice dropped to almost a whisper. "The chances of that must be very small."

She spun toward Peter and grabbed his shoulders. Her eyes lit up with a wild energy. "When did you say Clare was here?" she asked.

Peter tried to take a step back, but Ann held him tight.

"*When was she here?*" asked Ann.

"Two weeks ago, I think."

The Bureau of Farm Animal Accounting had fallen three weeks ago.

"It's a message!" shouted Ann. "Quicksort is a message!"

Comments and the Baker's Apprentice

Comments are additional text within code that can greatly improve the code's readability by providing additional insight, explanation, or summarization. For example, a comment before a large block of numeric statements might simply explain "Solve $a \cdot x^2 + b \cdot x + c = 0$ for x," allowing the user to understand exactly what the following block of code is meant to do.

❧

"NOW THIS IS HOW you write an algorithm," proclaimed Ann. After days of reading through some of the worst-written scrolls in the history of the kingdom, Clare's scroll on "The Application of QuickSort to Filing Expense Reports" provided a welcome change.

"How so?" asked Peter, leaning in to look at the scroll. He stared for a moment. "I guess it's nice handwriting," he said.

"It's so much more than that," said Ann. "The algorithm itself is readable. The variable names make sense, the functions are well defined, and there are comments. Good comments!"

"Comments?" asked Peter. "That seems unnecessary. I thought a good algorithm was supposed to make sense on its own."

"Not always," said Ann. "In complex algorithms, good comments can help make everything more understandable. Other times, a good comment can provide useful insights into why an approach was used."

Ann paused as she thought back. "Our castle's baker, Breadtista, was the first person to show me the importance of a good comment. I spent a summer as his apprentice. In fact, I spent a lot of summers apprenticing; my father is a fan of a broad education. Anyway, as part of his world-renowned teaching program, Breadtista insisted that each apprentice thoroughly document his or her work. All recipes, tips, and tricks must be clearly documented to create a reference that lives beyond the apprenticeship."

"Why make every apprentice repeat the work?" asked Peter. "Breadtista could simply copy his best recipes, right?"

"Learning to write a good recipe is part of the education. As Breadtista often pointed out, the key to a great recipe is capturing the perfect amount of information. Where other bakers wrote recipe books filled with lists of bland instructions, such as 'Add two eggs and blend well,' Breadtista insisted on adding comments to his recipes. He used wonderful comments that added context and the perfect amount of explanation."

Peter looked unconvinced. In his time as the librarian's apprentice, he couldn't remember a single instance when he had needed additional context. When the master librarian gave instructions, Peter wrote them down verbatim.

"Here," said Ann as she pulled an old notebook out of her bag. "Here's Breadtista's recipe for his famous eight-chili strawberry muffins."

Step 5: Cut the strawberries into cubes of 1 cm per side. [This size allows the flavors to blend while preserving the fruit's texture.]
Step 6: Add the strawberries to the dough.
Step 7: Gently stir until the strawberries are mixed into the dough.

"The comments have the brackets around them," explained Ann, pointing at the symbols "[" and "]."

"I guess it's useful to know why the strawberries should be that size," said Peter. "How else do you use comments? Can you provide information about how you thought up a recipe?"

Ann shook her head adamantly. "Comments should always provide information meaningful to the recipe itself. Breadtista would rant for hours about recipe books by famous castle chefs that contained thirty-page digressions on the author's lifelong quest for the perfect pancake. He considered it especially egregious if the recipe then produced chewy pancakes. As he would say: 'Pancakes should not be chewy, and comments should not be life stories.' He felt strongly about it."

"Did it take you long to learn to write good comments?" asked Peter.

Ann started laughing. "It took me a month to write any comments at all. I didn't see the use of them. I'd complain and say things like 'I won't forget what I did' and 'Isn't that step obvious?' I was such a pain.

"But Breadtista was patient. He would always give the same answer: 'Just because it's obvious to you at this moment doesn't mean you won't forget it, or that someone else won't need an explanation when they read the recipe.' He gave a very logical argument, but I still ignored it.

"Then Breadtista found the perfect way to reinforce the importance of *good* comments. He started making me work from the worst notes of previous students. It was agonizing. Sometimes I had no idea what the instructions meant. Other times, they went on forever."

Ann flipped a few pages back in her notebook. "Look at this mess!"

Step 1: Measure out 1/4 of an ounce of yeast into a small bowl. [We put it into a bowl so that we can add water in step 2 to activate the yeast.]
Step 2: Add two tablespoons of warm water to the bowl with the yeast. [We add the water to the bowl in order to activate the yeast.]
Step 3: Wait 5 minutes. [We wait 5 minutes in order to

```
allow the yeast to activate in the water.]
```

"A third-year apprentice wrote that recipe," Ann explained. "It was horrible. I never made it past step 85 in that recipe. In fact, I 'accidentally' spilled a full pitcher of water over the parchment so as to spare anyone else from reading it."

Ann sighed. "After that, I learned the value of good comments. It turns out that nothing reinforces the concept of understandable, well-documented recipes more than having to read other people's recipes."

"And the quicksort scroll?" asked Peter, returning to the topic at hand.

"Well-commented," answered Ann with a smile.

"Sure. But does it have the information you need?"

Ann looked worried. "Is has some of it—a direction at least. We still have so much work to do. But I fear we don't have much time left."

The Curse of Excessive Commenting

Good comments can improve the readability of code. However, over-commenting can do the opposite. Unnecessary comments waste both space and the reader's attention without adding value.

❧❧❧

THE NEW ATHENS BLACKSMITH, Drex, had been cursed. Drex freely admitted that he had provoked the wizard Marcus, but the curse seemed like an extreme reaction. The wizard could have simply insulted him back or walked away. There were plenty of reasonable options. He didn't have to curse Drex.

As much as the curse annoyed Drex, his apprentice Rachel suffered more. The Curse of Excessive Commenting was designed to annoy both the teacher and the student. Whenever Drex explained something, he now did it in excruciating detail.

"Watch how I form this hinge," Drex instructed. "First I pick up the metal with these large tongs. They are made of a heavier metal, so they won't burn or melt in the fire. Then I use the tongs to put metal in the fire, where it will heat up."

As he spoke, Drex grabbed a small blob of metal with his tongs and shoved it into the fire. After a moment, he felt obligated to add, "I'm still heating it up in the fire." He reiterated this observation five more times before the metal was hot enough to work.

"Now, I use the hammer to flatten the metal," Drex explained. "I'm hitting the metal with the hammer. I'm hitting it again. I'm hitting it again."

Rachel stood off to the side, watching. After the tenth repetition of "I'm hitting it again," she rolled her eyes. Not only were these descriptions annoying, but it also made it hard for her to follow what was going on. Drex narrated at such a low level that it was difficult to pay attention to the high-level flow. The constant stream of tiny details overran the concept of forming the hinge.

"I'm hitting it again," narrated Drex.

The first time Drex had described the process of making a hinge, it had been simple. He had described the entire first ten minutes of work as: "First, flatten out a small piece of metal." That was all. He had left unspoken the low-level details that any blacksmith should easily pick up: to flatten metal you heat it and hit it with a hammer.

"I'm hitting it again," narrated Drex.

The commentary was driving Rachel crazy. She thought back bitterly to the encounter with the wizard three days ago. Drex had confronted Marcus to complain about his magic candle. The candle had burned out, which magic candles should never do. When Drex had discovered that the wizard's apprentice had created the candle, he had made the fateful mistake of insulting Marcus's teaching skills. "At least I tell my apprentices what they need to know," Drex had bragged. It turned out to be a mistake to taunt a sleep-deprived wizard at two in the morning.

"I'm hitting it again," narrated Drex.

At least Marcus wasn't evil. He had placed only a temporary curse on Drex, forcing him to overcomment on all of his actions for the next week.

"I'm hitting it again," narrated Drex.

Unfortunately, Rachel didn't know if she could last another four days.

Data Structures for Research

Data structures can often be used as core elements of complex algorithms. In these cases, data structures do more than just store data. They organize the data and help make operations, such as finding a specific value, efficient.

❦

"YOU WANT THEM RIGHT here?" asked Peter. He motioned toward a tall stack of books. He had serious doubts about the pile's stability.

"On top," said Ann without looking up. "I should also have some more requests in a minute."

"Are you sure you want them on top?"

Ann looked up in surprise. "Of course I'm sure. I have a system."

"A system?" asked Peter. "It looks more like a stack of books. I think it would make more sense if I put the new books on the bottom. I keep putting new books on top, and the early books keep getting buried deeper."

Ann considered the pile for a moment. It now contained at least fifty books and was beginning to lean dangerously to one side.

"It's a stack," Ann said.

"I can see that," said Peter. "I helped stack them. Wouldn't it help to organize them? It might be more efficient."

"You don't understand. It's a computational stack—a last-in, first-out data structure. It's organized."

"How is that pile *organized*?" asked Peter in disbelief.

"The most recently requested books are on top," answered Ann. Then, after a moment, she set her pen down and turned her full attention to Peter. "Everyone has their own way of doing research. Some people like to try a bunch of different ideas at the same time. Some people jump around. I use depth-first search."

"What does depth-first search have to do with research?"

"I keep going deeper and deeper into a subject until I hit a dead end. Then I backtrack and try something different. A stack is perfect for that type of research.

"Consider the books that you just brought up: *On the Use of Dice for Selecting Random Numbers in the Range of 1 to 6* and *Advanced Probability for the Study of Garden Gnomes*. Both books are related to the topic that I read about a few minutes ago—the use of randomness in certain algorithms. So I decided to dig deeper into randomness. Next, I'll take one of those two books off the top of the stack, read it, and possibly ask for other related books.

"As I finish with books, I take them off the stack. This means that when I hit a dead end in one of my investigations, I find older books that are lower in the stack. My research automatically backtracks to earlier ideas."

Peter nodded intently. "What a great data structure!" he exclaimed. "It keeps your information organized exactly as you need it. It's efficient, too! Inserting and removing books are both $O(1)$ operations; you put new books on top and take books off the top. No need to sort anything. It's amazing."

"I guess so," Ann agreed. "For the record, the insertion operation is called 'push' and the removal operation is called 'pop.' You push data onto a stack and pop it off."

"Did you develop this data structure yourself?"

Ann looked confused. "A stack of books? I doubt it. I'm quite confident that people have been putting books into piles for a long time."

"Oh, right." Peter paused. "Why are you researching randomness, anyway?"

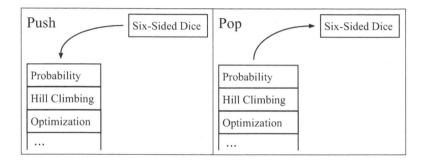

"I'm not sure," Ann admitted. "I got the idea from this magic purse that I was given. It magically tracks how much money is in it."

Ann showed Peter the purse from Marcus. She took a dime out, and the counter decreased by $0.10.

"What does that have to do with anything?" asked Peter.

Ann shrugged. "Since I left on my journey, the value has slowly trended downward. During any given week it bounces up and down, but the long-term trend is the same. Something about that reminded me of randomized algorithms. They randomly explore different solutions, always trying to find something better."

Peter looked back and forth between Ann and the purse. "I still don't get it."

"It's a long shot," admitted Ann. "But something about Clare's message made me think of the purse. As I said, I keep following one idea deeper and deeper until I hit a dead end."

Peter looked down at the stack of books and shuffled uncomfortably. "But do you have time for that? For dead ends, I mean."

"I don't know," answered Ann honestly.

"And what if you're right?" asked Peter, sounding more worried.

"We win," answered Ann. "That would be a good thing."

"But the wizard will still be there. He'll probably be a few feet away by the time you try your idea. Couldn't he just cast a giant fireball at us?"

"This wizard doesn't really seem to be the fireball type," offered Ann.

"How about a different curse then? What about boils?"

"I think I have an idea about that too," Ann said. "If the NP-hard curse is as powerful as I think it is, he needs to use a lot of magic. As long as we can avoid being cursed by the first spell, we should be safe from any followup spells for a while."

"Are you sure?" asked Peter.

"No. But all evidence seems to point that way."

Peter nodded to himself a few times. Then, reaching some internal conclusion, he turned and walked purposefully toward the library's main doors.

"Where are you going?" Ann asked. She wondered if she had managed to frighten him into running. Admittedly, fleeing in terror would actually be the safest course of action for him.

"To make a new friend," said Peter. "If your research works out and we avoid the curse and the wizard doesn't have enough magic left to smite us with a fireball, then we could use some more help. And if your research doesn't work out, I guess it doesn't matter anyway."

After he left, Ann looked back at the stack of books. She tried to push all of those 'ands' out of her mind and focus on the research at hand. She still needed to figure out how to avoid being cursed in the first place. She carefully reached over and popped the next book of the stack.

Expected Running Time

The expected running time of an algorithm indicates how long an algorithm will take on average. This gives an indication of how the algorithm will perform on typical problems. However, unlike worst-case analysis, the expected running time can be optimistic for difficult instances.

❧

A WIZARD IN A DARK black cloak stood at the foot of the library stairs. In his right hand, he held a solid wooden staff carved with mathematical symbols. A large hood obscured his face.

"Good morning. I am looking for Peter," announced the wizard. He stopped at the foot of the steps and looked up at the two kids standing there.

Peter didn't answer. He gripped Ann's arm tightly and took a half step backward. "Are you sure about your plan?" he asked Ann in a whisper.

Ann looked at the wizard standing at the foot of the library steps. "No," she whispered back truthfully. "But we're out of time. This is our only option."

"We could run," offered Peter.

Ann didn't respond. She stared at the wizard, waiting for the spell to come.

The wizard cleared his throat loudly. He looked mildly annoyed that he didn't seem to have their full attention.

"Excuse me. Are you Peter?" the wizard asked again as he

started to approach. "I have a problem for which I need your help. I have been told that you are a great computational mind."

Peter's grip tightened.

"Ask *me*," Ann said.

The wizard paused and studied Ann for a moment. Then, he pulled back his hood. His face reminded Ann of any of the many tenured professors at her school. His gray hair barely covered his head and deep wrinkles adorned his face, but his eyes blazed intensely. He gave her a wicked smile. "Princess Ann? What a truly pleasant surprise. I had not expected to run into you so soon. Of course, I had hoped our paths would indeed cross."

"Are you going to ask me a question or not?" asked Ann.

The wizard's smile widened to consume his entire face. "Let's talk about a little problem that I call the traveling salesman problem. I need to find a fast, exact algorithm to solve that very problem on large graphs." His voice was calm and almost soothing; it reminded Ann of countless lectures that had put her to sleep. As he spoke, his right hand began to wave his staff back and forth. A faint blue glow emanated from the top.

"I was always partial to an algorithm that I learned in the sixth grade: randomized hill-climbing," stated Ann.

The wizard paused, looking confused. "Randomized hill-climbing?" he asked.

"It's quite simple," explained Ann. "Start with a guess at the solution. It will probably be wrong, but you can at least find out how good it is. In this case, guess a path and compute its total distance.

"Then, you start the optimization loop. At each step in the loop you:

1. Propose a small random change to your solution.
2. Check the new solution.
3. If the new solution is better, take it. If it isn't better, then take it with some small probability. I like to roll two six-sided dice and take a bad move if I roll a double six.

"You always take a move that will improve things. And

sometimes you take a move that makes things worse, so that you can ultimately find better solutions."

The wizard stared at Ann with his mouth open. Ann noticed a small bead of sweat on his forehead. "That's a heuristic algorithm—a series of guesses! It doesn't guarantee that you'll find the solution. It searches almost blindly."

"That's true," Ann agreed. "But it can do reasonably well most of the time."

"*Most* of the time?" asked the wizard.

"Surely you know that there are no efficient, exact algorithms for NP-hard problems... yet. In fact, there might not be *any* efficient solutions. No one knows. *But* some algorithms perform quite reasonably on most cases."

The wizard took a step back and raised his staff. "What trickery is this?" he asked.

"No trickery," answered Ann. "It's the same thinking as expected-time algorithm analysis. Worst-case performance of algorithms only tells you part of the story. My kindergarten teacher once learned that the hard way when she—"

"Enough!" the wizard bellowed.

Ann smiled back condescendingly. "It seems that you underestimated the full range of computational analysis at my disposal. There's a new world of analysis where algorithms and probability meet. Your curse has no power there."

"You have to be a world expert in heuristic algorithms and expected running times for this spell to have no effect," objected the wizard. "How did you know?"

"I found a few clues along the way," Ann said.

"This is not over!" the wizard shouted.

He turned to leave—but found Terrible Todd blocking his retreat. The candlemaker's apprentice grinned as he grabbed the wizard by the arms and lifted him. Ann had no doubt that he could detain the wizard a day or two until Marcus and Sir Galwin arrived. And there was clearly no need to worry about Todd falling victim to the NP-hard curse.

"Yeah, it *is* over," shouted Peter, as he peeked out from behind Ann. Then more quietly, he mumbled, "Totally worth giving up my season tickets." He sounded as though he was still trying to convince himself.

The wizard spun back to Ann. "I am just the beginning," he proclaimed.

"The beginning of what?" asked Ann.

The old wizard laughed. "Chaos will engulf the entire kingdom. The computational foundations will crumble. It will be a new dark age."

"Why?" asked Ann.

"The first step in taking over, of course," said the wizard simply. The bluntness caught Ann off-guard. He continued, "Do you think your computational rule will last forever? I am just the beginning. Even if you break the kingdom's computational thinkers from my spell, do you think you're prepared for the challenges ahead?"

To everyone's surprise, Ann shrugged. "Who knows? I expect that I'll do well most of the time."

Returning Home

O NE YEAR AFTER SHE ventured forth to stop the darkness, Ann returned home to the castle. Trumpets announced her arrival, banners flew from every post, and a full honor guard lined her path. The castle had prepared a hero's welcome. A year ago, Ann would have been thrilled at this celebration. Now, she just wanted to sleep.

Ann proceeded directly to the throne room. Her father waited there, alone. He smiled proudly as she entered the room.

"I have stopped the darkness," Ann declared. "Or, at least, I've stopped the wizard who was trying to plunge the kingdom into a computational dark age. Marcus is still traveling around and undoing the damage."

"You did well," the king declared. "I am very proud of you. Welcome home, Ann."

"Thank you" was all that Ann could manage. A small doubt continued to nag at her. She tried to push it down and bask in her success, but it refused to be quiet.

King Fredrick noticed the look on her face. "What is wrong? You succeeded."

"I know," answered Ann. "It's just ..." She trailed off.

Her father waited for her to finish.

"What if I hadn't succeeded?" Ann asked, letting a flood of doubts rush out. "I came so close to failing. I'm not sure why it had to be me on this quest. I wasn't prepared at all."

Her father sat silently, watching her. After a moment, he spoke. "That is why it had to be you; you had to learn. To be precise, the seer said that it needed to be the person of my choice who would venture forth alone. I believed that you could use the experience. And, anyway, you were not paying attention during the prophecy."

Ann was shocked at this revelation. "What if I had failed?"

"I had confidence in you," he said calmly. "Some things have to be learned through practice and application. It is not enough to read about the concept of quests; you must go out and apply them. You must experiment with techniques through trial and error."

Ann didn't look convinced.

The king grew serious. "Listen carefully, Ann. When you take the throne, there will always be new challenges. Some will be easier and some will be more difficult, but you must face them all. The fate of the kingdom will depend on you again and again."

She nodded, but the doubt continued to eat at her. "What if I can't handle them? What if I'm not smart enough?"

"Some of the building blocks you have already; others, you will learn. It is up to you to continue to learn how to apply them."

Ann left the throne room with a sense of unease. She was safe at home. She had succeeded in her quest; she had saved the kingdom from plunging into a computational dark age. She knew that she should be happy.

Yet the encounter with the wizard still haunted her. Despite having stopped him, she had no clue as to his full motivations. What did he mean that he was "just the beginning"?

As Ann walked down the hall, her mind drifted back to the words of both the wizard and her father. There would always be more challenges to face.

Acknowledgements

A tremendous thanks goes out to all of the people who read earlier versions of this book and provided valuable feedback: Tim Bell, Abbi Bull, John Bull, Meg Bull, Edith Kubica, Regan Lee, Pat Stephenson, Kristen Stubbs, and Phil Wagner. Thanks to everyone who supported the earlier online version of these stories, and in particular to Eleanor Rieffel and Kristen Stubbs for their support in publicizing the stories. Thank you to my editor, Marjorie Carlson, whose help was critical. Thank you to Meagan O'Brien for her wonderful cover design. A deep thank you to my family for their support.

About the Author

Jeremy Kubica began his career in computer science by learning to program a Commodore in the second grade. There he soon mastered the secret arts of variables and loops—skills that helped propel him toward fame and ever greater challenges.

He has a B.S. in Computer Science from Cornell University and a Ph.D. in Robotics from Carnegie Mellon University. He spent his graduate school years creating algorithms to detect killer asteroids (actually stopping them was, of course, left as 'Future work').

He is the author of the Computational Fairy Tales blog.

Made in the USA
Middletown, DE
10 April 2017

42398822R00114